Other Avon Books in
ISAAC ASIMOV'S ROBOTS IN TIME *Series*
by William F. Wu

PREDATOR
MARAUDER

Coming Soon
DICTATOR

ISAAC ASIMOV'S
ROBOTS
IN TIME™

WARRIOR

WILLIAM F. WU

Databank by Matt Elson

A Byron Preiss Book

AVONOVA

AVON BOOKS • NEW YORK

ISAAC ASIMOV'S ROBOTS IN TIME: WARRIOR is an original publication of Avon Books. This work has never before appeared in book form. This work is a novel. Any similarity to actual persons or events is purely coincidental.

An Isaac Asimov's Robot City book.

AVON BOOKS
A division of
The Hearst Corporation
1350 Avenue of the Americas
New York, New York 10019

First AvoNova Printing: October 1993

AVONOVA TRADEMARK REG. U.S. PAT. OFF. AND IN OTHER COUNTRIES, MARCA REGISTRADA, HECHO EN U.S.A.

Printed in the U.S.A.

RA   10   9   8   7   6   5   4   3   2   1

This novel is dedicated to

Daniel Carnahan,

who will understand Marcus's dilemma.

Special thanks are due in writing this novel to Ricia Mainhardt, John Betancourt, and Byron Preiss.

Additional help during the period in which this was written came from Michael D. Toman, Laura J. LeHew, and Bridgett and Marty Marquardt.

Steve Chang followed Jane Maynard into the office of Mojave Center Governor, the gestalt robot who was supposed to be running the underground city of Mojave Center. Now the office was temporarily occupied by R. Hunter, the robot who had been specifically designed and built to lead the search for the missing Governor Robot.

"Good morning," said Hunter. "I trust your breakfast was good." He was already standing, six and a half brawny feet of humaniform robot in a northern European physiognomy now, with short blond hair and blue eyes, though he could change his shape and appearance at will. "Steve, Jane—this is Professor Gene Titus, our historian on the team for this mission."

"Pleased to meet you both." Gene was a tall, pleasant-looking man, only a little older than Steve, with bushy brown hair. He smiled broadly as he shook hands with them. "I'm a specialist in Roman history, especially the early imperial period. From what Hunter tells me, this trip we're about to take should be quite an experience."

"We've done two of them already," said Jane. "There's nothing like it."

"Hi," said Steve. He hung back a little, waiting to see what sort of guy Gene would turn out to be.

"So Hunter was telling me." Gene turned to the weird object standing against the wall. "So these are two of the six gestalt robots we're looking for?"

Steve said nothing. This was Jane's specialty.

"That's right," said Jane. "Mojave Center Governor split into his six component robots and these are the two we have brought back from the past so far."

"And so what is this, exactly?"

"This thing in front of us is what MC 1 and 2 look like, physically merged and shut down. If we get the other four back here to merge with them, we'll have MC Governor put back together again. At that point, he'll actually be humaniform."

"Not 'if' we bring them back," said Hunter soberly. "*When* we bring them back."

Steve grinned. "That's the right spirit. But, if you don't mind my asking . . ."

"Yes?"

"You look kind of young to be a professor."

"I just received my first position this year. My doctoral degree is so new, the ink's wet." He winked.

Jane laughed.

"I see." Steve smiled too, pleased at Gene's casual attitude. He had expected Gene to be a little more stuffy in his manner.

Gene turned to Jane. "Hunter has only started to brief me. You're the roboticist?"

"That's right."

"Then I guess you can explain something to me. The Laws of Robotics must be dictating the robots' behavior somehow, but I don't quite see the connection."

"Hunter, do you want to finish the briefing? Or does it matter?"

"Go ahead," said Hunter. His manner was serious and direct, telling Steve that he did not want to waste time with unnecessary talk.

"The Third Law of Robotics says, 'A robot must protect his own existence as long as such protection does not conflict with the First or Second Law,'" said Jane.

"What about it?" Gene asked.

"MC Governor is one of a small number of experimental Governor Robots that were being tested recently. All the others have malfunctioned. The Governor Robot Oversight Committee, for whom Hunter is working, needs to get hold of MC Governor to find out what may have happened to them all. MC Governor has split into his component robots and fled. Without interviewing him, I can only surmise his reasons, but I believe that under the Third Law, he split to avoid experiencing the same malfunction as the other Governor Robots. Also under the same Law, I think he fled in order to avoid being dismantled during a study of the problem."

"I see. So that's why they fled to different times in history." Gene nodded soberly. "I've already given Hunter my promise to keep the existence of time travel confidential. If time travel became widespread, history would be very vulnerable to all the people who might change it. But do the other Laws apply to the robots' decision to flee?"

"Oh, yes. The component robots miniaturized themselves to microscopic size when they used the time travel device. Their intention was to avoid receiving any instructions from humans—in the case of MC 1, who went back to the dinosaur age, he was anticipating survival into the human era. The Second Law of Robotics says, 'A robot must obey the orders given it by human beings except where such orders would conflict with the First Law.' "

"And if humans couldn't see the robots, they wouldn't give them any orders."

"That's the idea," said Steve.

"Then what's the problem?" Gene looked back and forth between Jane and Hunter.

"There are two problems," said Hunter. "The first is that the miniaturization process was flawed. All the component robots return to full size at some point back in history, without their desire or control. When they do this, they begin to interact with humans. Since they have to obey human orders, they may change history. Even worse, their obedience to the First Law of Robotics might even guarantee that they will make certain changes."

"The First Law says, 'A robot may not injure a human being, or, through inaction, allow a human being to come to harm,' " said Jane.

"Yes, I see the connection," said Gene.

"I arranged hypnotic sleep courses in Latin and ancient German for Steve and Jane," said Hunter. "In the case of German, we had to use a probable reconstruction of the language based on what our finest linguist robots could surmise. I assume it went well?"

"*Adfirmo*," said Jane, smiling. "I affirm."

"We won't really know until we try speaking to the natives," said Steve.

"Gene, were you able to use the lesson packages I sent you when we made our arrangements?" Hunter asked.

"Yes. I used them while I slept on the plane on my way here. The flight wasn't as long as a good night's sleep, but I concentrated on the German since I already had to learn Latin as part of my education."

"Excellent. I have accessed these languages thoroughly myself. Now, then. I have arranged for a Security detail to take all of us to Room F-12 of the Bohung Institute. I left your clothing and lapel pin radios there during the night, after I received them from the robots who made them."

"You still want me to review them for authenticity?" Gene asked. "You mentioned that when you first contacted me."

"Definitely," said Hunter. "Let us go."

Hunter was deliberately keeping the tension he felt from the humans. The First Law imperative was driving him hard to get back into the past as fast as possible, but of course he knew that all of the team's preparations had to be made first. Now, as he led the humans out of the office to the waiting Security vehicle, he opened his internal communication link to the city computer.

"Please contact all the members of the Governor Robot Oversight Committee in a conference call."

"Acknowledged," said the city computer.

Hunter felt that his responsibilities to the Committee required that he report on the progress of his missions. However, he had not shared with them the fact that time travel was involved. If the ability to travel through time were to become widely known and used, the potential harm to humans would be immense. His judgment of how to follow the First Law in this matter therefore prevented him from explaining the details to the Committee. He also wanted to confer with them alone, so that the human members of his team would not mistakenly reveal the existence of time travel.

The team rode the electric cart silently down the broad, clean thoroughfares of Mojave Center. Around them, robots and humans pursued their daily routines, unaware that in the Bohung Institute, the first and only device for time travel was among them. The underground city, beneath the Mojave Desert in California, remained calm and safe.

"Have you briefed Gene about Wayne Nystrom?" Steve asked Hunter.

"Not yet," said Hunter.

"That name is familiar to me," said Gene. "Has he been in the news or something?"

"Not lately," said Jane. "But from time to time, he has appeared in the scientific news because of his advances in robotics. He invented the Governor Robots."

"Is he going to be joining the team?" Gene asked.

"I wish." Steve grinned and shook his head. "He's operating on his own, trying to get the component robots away from us. He wants to conduct his own investigation of their malfunction, without us."

"His own? Is he able to go back in time, too?"

"Up to now," said Steve.

"What do you mean?"

Steve looked at Hunter. "You know the technicalities better than I do."

"I do not know all the particulars myself," said Hunter. "However, Dr. Nystrom has appeared in the past during both of our previous missions."

"Does he have a second time travel device?"

"No," said Hunter. "The device we have all used was initially created by MC Governor, accomplished by modifying an existing piece of research equipment. The component robots all used it, and Wayne Nystrom followed them, preceding us. We were the last to use it."

"You didn't get hold of him when he returned to this time?" Gene was puzzled.

"No. On our first mission, I did not realize he was a factor in this project," said Hunter.

"May I ask what happened, or is that prying?" Gene glanced at all three of the others, uncertainly.

"Of course you may ask," said Hunter. "You are part of the team. I had Security robots guard the Institute and stationed a robot just outside the door. Wayne apparently returned from the Late Cretaceous to Room F-12 and quickly reprogrammed the console to send him back to the time of Captain Henry Morgan. That's where we became aware of him next."

"And now?"

"When we returned, I moved a robot named Ishihara to the inside of the room with orders to apprehend Wayne and to report to me when he appeared."

"But Nystrom hasn't come back?"

"No," said Hunter.

"What about that, Hunter?" Steve asked. "Do you think he's still back in Morgan's time, in the 1600s? Now that we have MC 2 safely here, maybe we should go after Wayne."

"He has no reason to remain there," said Hunter. "And from what I can tell, our history has not been changed except in regard to the explosions. I believe he may have some other plan in mind that is beyond my anticipation for now. So our best plan of action is to continue our mission to recover MC 3, as planned."

"Explosions?" Gene eyed Hunter carefully. "I caught a news item on my way here about a mysterious explosion in Germany—come to think of it, in the general area we're about to visit. Is there a connection?"

"That is correct," said Hunter. "When the component robots reach the approximate time from which they first journeyed back into the past—in other words, about now—they explode with nuclear force. This is caused by the instability in their atomic structure caused by the flawed miniaturization. The destruction to human life acts as a First Law imperative on me."

"I get it," Gene said grimly. "We have to go back and get that one right now. That's MC 3?"

"You are correct again," said Hunter.

All night, while he had prepared the clothing and new communicators for the team, he had monitored the news. Millions were dead in northwestern Germany, just east of the Ems River and the Weser River, in a heavily populated industrial area. The radiation was beginning to spread over most of Europe. Worst

of all, some news analysts were concerned that ter-
rorists might be attempting to disrupt world peace.
Hunter feared that old, mutual fears and accusations
by different nations could cause additional violence.
The First Law required that he eliminate the cause of
the explosion without delay.

The Security vehicle pulled up in front of the Bohung
Institute. Hunter led the team silently inside the building, through the robot Security detail guarding it. He
had arranged to shut down the Institute as soon as he
had realized the importance of the experimental time
travel device that MC Governor had created.

Inside, Hunter took his team to Room F-12 and
introduced Gene to Ishihara. This large room housed
an opaque sphere about fifteen meters in diameter.
The remainder of the room was lined with countertops,
most of them occupied with computers, monitors, a
communications console, and miscellaneous office
items. Clothing was stacked on one counter near the
door to an adjacent room.

Ishihara passed out oral vaccines to the humans,
which Hunter had chosen and requisitioned during
the night. These vaccines could not guarantee protection from disease, because the modern microbes
had mutated considerably in the millennia that had
passed since Roman times, but Hunter knew they
would improve the humans' chances of avoiding serious illness. The humans took them immediately.

Ishihara waited impassively by the door. Everyone
turned to Hunter for instructions. He pointed to the
stack of clothing he had left earlier.

"Gene, please examine the clothing for authenticity," said Hunter. "You will find tunics, heavy cloaks,

and boots for male costumes; Jane has a full-length gown, cloak, and boots. If you pass them, Steve will look them over to make sure they are sturdy and practical enough."

"And here are our new communicator pins," said Jane, picking up small silver broaches. She held one out to Gene, showing him the button to be pressed to activate the radio. "We can use them to hold our cloaks on."

"That is my intention," said Hunter. "When the clothing has been approved, take turns changing in the adjacent room."

Hunter received a message through his internal link. "City computer calling R. Hunter."

"Hunter here." While the humans examined their new clothes, he would have time to respond without disturbing them.

"I have the Governor Robot Oversight Committee on a conference call for you.

"Please connect me."

Instantly, the four faces of the Committee members appeared on his internal video screen in split portrait shots. Everyone exchanged polite, perfunctory greetings. Then Hunter got to the point.

"I am pleased to report that MC 2 is safely in custody," said Hunter.

"Excellent," said Dr. Redfield, the pretty blonde. "Where did you find him?"

"In the West Indies," said Hunter. He decided not to mention Jamaica, because that would set a precedent of being specific. Being vague with the Committee was the only way to avoid having to tell them, sooner or later, about the time travel device. "He is well, but has been instructed to merge with MC 1 and shut down. They are in a secure location."

"You've been very efficient," said Professor Post, scratching his black beard thoughtfully. "Do you know where you will find your next quarry?"

"I have a lead in Europe," said Hunter.

"Where?" Dr. Chin moved a strand of her long black hair away from her face. "Which country?"

"I do not have an exact location," said Hunter. That was technically true, since he had not yet heard a report on ground zero of the explosion and the coordinates he had obtained from the console of the time travel device did not match those of any known town or city. Still, he was aware that he was very close to telling them an outright lie.

"You have found the first two component robots in only a few days," said Dr. Khanna. "What is your estimate for completing your assignment?"

"I would be unwise to predict that I can apprehend each of the remaining component robots in only one day," said Hunter. "Matters have proceeded well so far, allowing me to move quickly. Still, the first two pursuits were quite different and I expect the remaining four to be very unpredictable as well."

"I understand," said Dr. Khanna.

"I'm sure we're all very impressed with your efficiency so far," said Dr. Redfield.

"I should begin the next mission," said Hunter. "If you have no more questions, I shall get started."

"Of course," said Professor Post. "Good luck."

Everyone signed off.

After Gene inspected each item of clothing, he passed it to Steve. Then Steve held it up, shook it loose, and tugged at the seams. Hunter had explained that they were going to a forested mountain area in autumn, the rainy season in northern Germany. They would need warm clothes. The cloaks and outer tunics were made of wool, while the undertunics were made of linen.

"Yours are fine," said Steve, handing Jane her outfit. She went to change first.

All the clothes passed inspection. When everyone had changed, Hunter passed each of the humans a small leather pouch filled with common Roman coins from the era to which they were going. All the communicator pins were in place, fastening the humans' cloaks at the neck.

"Well, Gene," said Jane. "I know you said the clothes are authentic—but how do we look?"

"You look perfect," said Gene. "As a matter of fact, you will look right at home in the mountains of central Europe in this period."

"We shall masquerade as traveling merchants," said Hunter, adjusting his own long brown cloak. Since his radio links were internal, he fastened his cloak with an ordinary silver pin. "I shall be somewhat vague in order to avoid being tripped up in a small mistake, but I shall present us as visitors from Roman Gaul seeking trade in silverwork with the German tribes across the Rhine."

"You have some?" Gene asked.

Hunter pointed to a leather bag, sitting on a counter where the clothing had been. "Each item inside is a relatively inexpensive piece of jewelry that I shall present as samples and gifts. None is authentic, but I had some of the robots here in Mojave Center develop them last night from authentic models. The metallic content and style of art and design are accurate. I believe that their presence in Roman Germany will not cause any alteration of history or culture. Gene, please look them over and see if you agree. Steve, the leather bag has a shoulder strap so you can carry the jewelry in it conveniently."

"Come to think of it, Hunter," Steve said with a grin, running a hand through his black hair, "that works for you three just fine. When we come into contact with Romans or Germans, how are you going to explain having someone of East Asian descent with you? We better have our story straight about who I am."

Hunter looked at Steve. His boots, tunic, and cloak were certainly acceptable, but he was right that his Chinese features would stand out in ancient Germany. "Gene, what do you suggest?"

"Well . . ." Gene thought a moment, looking up from

the jewelry box. "You know, even though Rome had no official contact with China, some Roman merchants were aware of Han Dynasty China. They traded through the Parthians for Chinese silk and sold it to the wealthiest Romans. So maybe Steve could be a slave who accompanied his merchant owners through the Parthian Empire with a load of silk and then was sold."

"Okay." Steve laughed. "If that will hold up with the Romans, it's good enough for me."

"Very well," said Hunter. "Gene, what do you think of the silverwork?"

"It looks fine to me," said Gene. "I'm not a specialist in Roman art as such, but I certainly don't see any glaring problems." He closed and latched the box.

"Good." Hunter looked at each of them. "Unless you have questions, I believe we are ready to go."

"This way." Steve picked up the leather bag. Then he slung the bag over his shoulder and moved to the big sphere that dominated the room. It was a solid metal globe fifteen meters in diameter. First he helped Jane and Gene climb inside. Then he followed, sliding down into the curved bottom with them.

Hunter set the coordinates and the timer on the console. When he had finished, he hoisted himself inside and closed the sphere. For a long moment, the team sat crowded together in the dark.

Steve felt himself land on hard, rocky ground. He pushed himself up and saw that Hunter, Jane, and Gene were doing the same. They were on a steep, grassy slope, in a dense forest. The leaves were an autumn blaze of orange, red, and yellow. Overhead, the sky was cloudy and gray. Steve smelled rain. Far below, he could see a gray river winding its way between the bluffs on each side of it, reflecting the subdued sunlight.

"Is that the Rhine?" Steve asked.

"The Weser River," said Hunter. "The Rhine is well west of here."

"This is quite a view." Steve got to his feet. The forest was full of both evergreens and hardwoods. "Well, Hunter? Where do we go?"

"We shall have to explore some," said Hunter. "In all likelihood, MC 3 will return to normal size out in the forest somewhere, which is most of the surrounding territory. According to the history I accessed through the city computer, the German tribes have a mixed economy, based on tilled fields, cattle, and hunting. Each tribe has a number of separate villages. Gene, does that match your information?"

"Yes, it does." Gene got to his feet and helped pull Jane up. "Generally speaking, they will be the ones who actually know the forest and routinely move through it."

"What about the Romans?" Jane straightened her gown. "They've conquered this area, as I understand it. Why aren't they going to be in the forest, too?"

"The Romans haven't really been here very long," said Gene. "They don't have a settled presence here, with families and merchants. All they really have is an army of occupation. They're outnumbered and limited in the range of territory they actually walk or ride through. In most cases, they will only march out in a troop large enough to defend itself."

"Come on, Hunter," said Steve impatiently. "Which way do we go?"

"I believe that friendly contact with the Germans will most likely facilitate our mission," said Hunter. "According to what you have said, Gene, do you agree?"

"Yes, I do," said Gene. "And they shouldn't be hard to locate. Instead of looking for them, I think that if we simply start hiking, then warriors, hunters, or sentries of the Cherusci tribe are likely to find us."

Hunter nodded and began to hike up the slope, eastward away from the Weser, pushing through thick branches. Jane and Gene followed in single file over the rocky ground. Steve deliberately took up the rear. After all, he had to look like their slave.

"Hey, Gene," Steve said, as they continued up the uneven slope. "Is all the country here this rough?"

"Most of it. This province goes east to the Elbe River and west to the Rhine. We're in the middle of it here. It's very mountainous, and many of the valleys are swamps. It includes part of modern Westphalia."

Up ahead, Hunter stopped at a small, level clearing. The three humans caught up to him. Steve could not see or hear any reason for them to have halted already.

"Nine humans are nearby," Hunter said quietly. "They are moving quietly, without speaking, ahead to our right. From the sound of their movements through the brush, I believe that they are still unaware of our presence. However, this is the contact we want."

"We don't want to be mistaken for deer and shot," said Steve. "Should we start talking loudly or something?"

"We shall start using Latin," said Hunter, switching to that language, "to support the idea that we have just

crossed over from Gaul. Stay close and keep talking."
He started walking again.

"Do you see anything yet?" Jane asked, trying out
her own Latin.

"*Specto*," said Hunter. "I am looking. So far, I can
only hear them. They are still at a distance that is
beyond human hearing, but they are drawing closer."

The forest was dense, with thick underbrush and
many fallen logs blocking their way. In the rare patches
of direct sunlight, the air was warm, but most of the
ground was shaded by the canopy of trees. Steve's
cloak kept snagging on branches until he got used
to keeping it pulled tightly against his body. In the
lead, Hunter, because of his height, found the going
slow as he worked his way through the tree branches.
Every so often, Gene leaned over and freed Jane's cloak
from a snag.

"*Veni, vidi, vici*," muttered Steve. "I'm a slave from
foreign parts. It's understandable if my Latin is bad,
right?"

"Yes, it is understandable," said Hunter, pushing
through some thick pine branches and holding them
back for the others. "But we should not be overheard
speaking English unless we simply cannot communicate our point to each other without it. Do continue
talking, however."

"Keep talking," Steve said cheerfully, in Latin. "Talk
so they know we're human and not tonight's dinner.
What shall we talk about?"

"Gene," said Jane. "Exactly who are these Germans,
anyway? Who's about to find us?"

"They're barbarian warriors," said Gene. "Semi-
pastoral nomads, technically. Right now, they aren't

really very different from the Gauls across the Rhine, but they will be."

"Hunter, are they any closer?" Jane asked. "You'll hear them before we will."

"I think they have heard us," said Hunter. "The pattern of their footsteps is changing. They have begun to spread out some as they approach us."

"Gaul on one side of the Rhine and Germany over here," said Steve. "France as opposed to Germany. That's centuries in the future, though." He stepped over a thick, exposed tree root. "Right?"

"Yes and no," said Gene. "Their divergent history has already begun. A generation ago, Julius Caesar established the Rhine River as the border between Roman-held Gaul and the land of the independent German tribes across it. In 9 B.C., the younger stepson of Caesar Augustus, a man named Drusus, invaded the land across the Rhine and pushed the border eastward to the Elbe River because it's a more defensible border from the Roman side. That's the territory where we are now." He paused to point out a slippery, moss-covered rock to Jane, who stepped over it.

"So it's a Roman province," said Steve.

"Well, so far. A Roman named Publius Quinctilius Varus is governor right now. He considers the province thoroughly subdued and is overconfident—to say the least—of his power." Gene held another branch back out of the way for Jane and Steve.

Ahead of them, Hunter had stopped for a moment, looking around carefully. "They are very close," he whispered in English. "I also hear the sound of small animals, probably hunting dogs." He began walking again.

Steve could not hear any sign of the other people. "Dogs? Why aren't they barking and howling and coming after us?"

"They're well trained," said Gene. "To flush game sometimes and to sneak up quietly at other times."

"Simply remain calm," Hunter said in Latin, this time in a normal tone. "Continue our conversation if you wish. Lower your voices, though, if you go on discussing history. We do not want to give our friends ideas they do not already have."

"Not much chance of that," said Gene. "These events are already in motion."

"What do you mean that this is a Roman province 'so far'?" Jane asked Gene.

"The province doesn't stay Roman very long," said Gene. "A German prince of the Cherusci tribe, called Arminius, has been granted Roman citizenship. He's been dealing with Varus in this new province, representing the Cherusci. In fact, the entire tribe has been given the privileged position of a federated state within the Roman Empire. For this reason, many of the Cherusci have Latin names, like Arminius himself."

"But what happened to the Romans?" Steve ducked under another low branch, hurrying to keep up. He looked around for the Germans that Hunter could hear, but still saw no direct sign of them. Then he noticed some birds suddenly fluttering out of a tree a short distance away. He realized that they might have been disturbed by humans walking near them.

"This year," said Gene, "Arminius leads an uprising against the Romans. The Cherusci Germans and some allied tribes ambushed Varus in the Teutoburger Forest, destroying him and his entire army. The Roman border will be pushed back to the Rhine until the Empire falls completely. As a result, Gaul will be culturally and linguistically Romanized to a degree that Germany never will be."

"What of it?" Steve demanded. "I mean, the Roman Empire was huge. This one province couldn't have meant that much to the Romans, could it?"

"Not to the living Roman Empire," said Gene. "But think of it this way. If this province had remained within the Roman Empire, then maybe more of Germany would have been conquered by the Romans. When the Roman Empire collapsed, the Germanic tribes that helped bring it down might have been culturally Latinized and much more like the tribes in Gaul, which became France, than the Germany of our history. The history of the new Germany would have been extremely different forever after, altering major world events in many different centuries."

"So the real difference would came later," said Steve. "I see."

"When was the ambush in Teutoburger Forest?" Hunter asked.

"It—" Gene stopped as an arrow whistled in front of Hunter and hit a tree trunk.

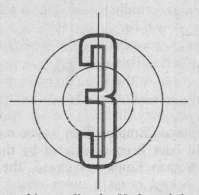

Hunter stopped immediately. He heard the humans on his team halt behind him. No one spoke.

Nine strange young men stepped into view. Some appeared in front of the team, while others moved out of the trees on each side. Black and gray dogs stepped out with them, their noses quivering. Hunter was alert for violence, the First Law dominating his thoughts.

None of the Germans was as tall as Hunter, but they were heavyset muscular men wearing fur tunics and leather leggings. All had long, shaggy hair. Most were blond, while a few had red hair. Each of them held a long, heavy spear. They carried bows on their shoulders; quivers of arrows and long knives hung on their belts.

Hunter waited patiently, neither speaking nor moving. A tall, hulking German with bushy red hair and a full beard that matched stepped up in front of Hunter. In addition to his weapons, he carried some sort of steer horn on a thong over his shoulder. While his companions held their spears ready for action, he rested the butt of his spear confidently on the ground. He looked over Hunter with quick blue eyes.

"Hail, strangers," the German said stiffly in Latin. "I am Vicinius, of the Cherusci. Who are you?"

"Hail, Vicinius," said Hunter. "I am called Hunter, but we are not hunting today. We seek the Cherusci tribe in friendship. You can see that we are unarmed." He turned and introduced the humans on the team by their first names.

Vicinius nodded politely to each of them, though his eyes widened slightly in surprise at the introduction of Jane. None of his companions lowered their spears. They did not smile or speak, either. Steve glanced at one who was glowering suspiciously at the group.

"You seek us?" Vicinius asked. "Why?"

"We come seeking friends with whom to trade," said Hunter. "We have only a few poor samples of gifts today, but now we seek friends for the future."

"Where are these gifts?" Vicinius glanced at all of them. "I see no packhorse."

Steve unslung the leather bag from his shoulder, expecting Hunter to call him forward.

"This is a poor place to talk," said Hunter. "May we find a spot that is more comfortable?"

Vicinius had glanced at Steve when he had shifted the leather bag, so the question about the presence of gifts was answered. Steve now realized that Hunter was angling for an invitation back to the home village of these hunters. Holding the bag uncertainly, he said nothing.

Vicinius seemed to understand Hunter's meaning, as well. He looked over the group again, appraising them. His companions waited for him to speak.

"Hunter," Gene said quietly, switching to English so the Germans could not understand. "I suggest some warrior-bonding. Compliment his weapons and his skill at arms. If he offers you a chance to show off, do well but don't embarrass him. And try speaking German to him."

"You have fine spears," said Hunter politely in German. "Your companions are all very fit."

"You speak our language." Vicinius smiled for the first time, looking Hunter in the eye again, and some of his companions murmured among themselves in surprise.

"We all speak it to some degree," said Hunter. "Vicinius, we have heard that the men of the Cherusci tribe are great hunters and warriors. As traders, we are impressed by this reputation. Would one of your party be so kind as to demonstrate this skill with weapons?"

Vicinius grinned in appreciation of this compliment, and so did some of his companions. He turned and looked around among the trees for a moment. Then he hefted his spear, reared back, and heaved it through the air.

The big spear flew among the leafy branches, somehow missing all of them, and struck a tree trunk about thirty-five yards away with a loud thunk.

Hunter estimated the weight of the spear from its appearance and the sound it had made striking the tree. The distance and the size of the target alone were not particularly impressive, but he could see that in this throw, Vicinius's challenge had been to throw the spear through the dense forest without hitting the many tree branches and underbrush that would have deflected the weapon from its target. He had accomplished the maneuver perfectly.

"Will you throw?" Vicinius gestured for one of his companions to offer a spear to Hunter.

Hunter accepted the spear. He wanted to make a good impression on these hunters and warriors but he remembered Gene's warning not to embarrass their host. Hunter carefully raised the spear and threw it at the same tree.

Hunter's spear also flew straight, missing all the surrounding branches, and struck the same tree trunk. However, it hit just below the first spear. The other warriors nodded their appreciation of his throw but said nothing.

Vicinius, however, laughed aloud. "Excellent! You must be a fine hunter."

"I have come to trade, not to hunt," said Hunter, in what he hoped was a modest tone of voice.

"And your friends?"

"Traders as well."

Vicinius nodded, looking them over again. He pointed to another of the warriors. That man also took a broad stance and cast his spear. It, too, sailed among the dense leaves and branches to strike a different tree trunk. He turned and grinned at Vicinius and Hunter.

"Very impressive," said Hunter.

Vicinius pointed to another warrior, then nodded toward Gene. The other man tossed his spear vertically to the surprised historian.

Steve stifled a laugh. "Good luck, Gene."

"I'll need it," said Gene, grinning. He moved up next to Hunter, where he had more open space, and carefully gripped the spear. "Well, I don't know about this."

"You can do it," said Jane.

"I wonder." Gene took a deep breath and imitated the stance he had seen the warriors take. Then he clenched his teeth and threw the spear.

It flew forward but, halfway to its target, the shaft of the spear grazed an overhanging branch and glanced off to the left. It fell out of sight in the underbrush.

All the Germans laughed. So did Steve. Gene shrugged, still smiling.

This time a warrior stepped up without bidding from Vicinius. He threw his spear as well, striking another tree near the first two that had spears hanging from them. The other warriors, now much more relaxed than they had been at first, cheered good-naturedly.

Another warrior tossed his spear to Steve, who caught it with his free hand.

"Uh-oh," said Steve, grinning as he set down the leather bag between his feet.

"You can't do much worse than I did," said Gene. "Go ahead. We're only traders, after all."

"Hey, I'm only a slave." Steve reared back like the others and threw the spear. It, too, clattered against some tree branches halfway to its target and fell out of sight. The warriors laughed, as did Jane and Gene.

Several of the warriors ran to fetch the spears.

"Don't I get a throw?" Jane asked, looking around at the other warriors.

"I'm afraid not," said Gene. "It's a cultural matter with them."

"Well, I probably wouldn't do any better than you two, anyway," said Jane.

"Those things are heavier than they look," said Steve. "I didn't know it was so hard." He picked up the leather bag again.

"You three have spirit," said Vicinius.

"We have more spirit than skill," said Hunter. "However, I thank you for the game."

"It is well," said Vicinius. "You said you were traders from Gaul?"

"That is right."

"In what do you trade?"

"Silverwork."

"Silver, eh?" Vicinius glanced at the leather bag. Then he looked at Hunter's face for a long moment. "Please come to our village. It is not far. You will be my guests."

"Thank you." Hunter knew that bringing strangers back to the village was an important decision. Vicinius might also be more cautious than usual because of the tension between the Romans and Germans now. However, the reason for his hesitation did not really matter.

Some of the other German warriors had already gone to fetch the spears. Then Vicinius waved once and turned to lead the way through the forest.

Hunter followed him, remaining back a short distance to stay with his team. They were much slower than the Germans. As they picked their way through the forest, Steve was the most surefooted.

"Hunter," Jane said quietly in English. "Something has occurred to me about the component robots."

He waited for her to come up next to him. Then they walked together. "What is it?"

"I simply can't believe that they have chosen when and where to go in the past purely by chance."

"You feel they have specific motives behind their choices?" Hunter asked.

"They must," said Jane. "Random flight would have taken them to many parts of the world, far from the centers of historical focus."

"Why did MC 1 choose to go to what would become Alberta in the Late Cretaceous?"

"I have no way of knowing about that," said Jane. "But Sir Henry Morgan was a historical figure, even though a minor one. And MC 3's flight to the border of the Roman Empire just can't be an accident."

"Why do you feel this way?"

"In both Morgan's time and especially now, most of the world was not well documented historically. The vast majority of land area is outside historical record. And most of the land within historical record does not have anything very significant occurring at any given time. For some reason, MC 2 and 3 chose to be in the area of recorded human history, even while intending to remain microscopic."

"They represent only two of the six component robots," said Hunter.

"I thought of that. As a roboticist, I was intrigued by this mystery, so before breakfast this morning, I got on the city computer. I found out that when MC Governor did certain tasks with the city, he sometimes delegated them to his component personalities."

Hunter turned to her in surprise, holding a pine branch out of the way for her. "How did you learn that?"

"I asked for any information that might help identify

the component robots' separate abilities, tendencies, or personalities." She took the branch from Hunter and in turn held it for Gene.

"I see," said Hunter. "I was focused on MC Governor as an integral individual first, who split up. I did not think to approach the component robots as individuals while MC Governor was still functioning."

"I found out that MC 1 specialized in the environmental impact of Mojave Center on the surrounding area," said Jane. "MC 2 specialized in general troubleshooting for MC Governor. MC 3 handled security concerns for Mojave Center. I'm sure these match up in some way with the places they chose to go." She stepped over a large, fallen tree trunk and caught her cloak on a short branch.

"What about the other three component robots?" Hunter stopped to pull her cloak free.

"I don't recall. I left my notes with my regular clothes back in Room F-12."

"You believe that these specialties reflect their choices of where and in what time period to hide?"

"Yes, even though they intended to remain microscopic forever. It may be a subliminal influence of their specialties, rather than part of their deliberate, rational thought. But if I can figure out what kind of influence MC 3's specialty, for instance, had on him, I might have a shortcut for finding him here."

"You say that MC 3 handled security matters for Mojave Center," Hunter said. "This strikes me as irrelevant to his presence here. Do you have any guess as to where he might be now, or where he would go here, with this information?"

"No," Jane said. "Not yet."

The Germans quietly led the way through the forest. Hunter saw that they were still carefully watching the birds in the trees and stopping occasionally simply to listen. The dogs, too, were on the alert. He decided that they were still hoping to find prey for dinner, even on their way home.

Dr. Wayne Nystrom squatted next to a cold, fast-flowing stream in the forest. He drank some water out of his cupped hand and wiped his hand on a patch of grass. Then he shivered in the chilly breeze and looked around at the trees. A few birds chirped and twittered in the branches. Otherwise, the forest looked the same in every direction.

"I'm freezing," he muttered to himself. He stood up and slowly turned around again, hoping to see a sign of human life somewhere. The view, however, was the same now that he was standing as it had been when he was squatting.

Wayne had been lost ever since his arrival here. All he knew about his location was that he was somewhere in the German forest east of the Rhine in A.D. 9. He had no idea where to find human habitation.

Only a few hours ago by his own time, but seventeen centuries in the future from this year, he had taken some time to tinker with his belt unit. This was the device that he carried to trigger the time travel sphere back in Room F-12 of the Bohung Institute. In working with it, he had learned that it could control the settings in the console of the sphere even when he was in another time. This occurred during the early stage of its function, just before the sphere picked him up to move him through time. Instantly, he had realized that he could use this capability to his own advantage.

First he had used the unit's controls to slow down the action of the device. This had allowed him enough time to monitor and read all the records inside the console that ran the sphere. Since these records contained each setting that had been used so far, they told him where all the other component robots had gone. At the time Wayne read them, Hunter and his team had not used the sphere since going to Jamaica in 1668.

Based on when each of the component robots had left its own time, Wayne had judged that of the remaining component robots still at large, the one here in Germany was due to explode the soonest. Guessing that Hunter would try to capture him next, Wayne had also picked this location. If at all possible, he wanted to grab MC 3 and study him here in this time, before Hunter could take him back.

He had arrived safely, but moving directly from Jamaica in the summer of 1668 left him unprepared for life in this forested mountain area in central Europe. The water in the stream was clear and certainly untouched by industrial pollution, but finding food in this northern forest was going to require more work than buying tropical fruit in Port Royal, Jamaica. Worst of all, without heavier clothing, he might not survive the night. He was not sure how cold these mountains would get at night.

Rubbing his arms, he stood up and looked around. All he could do was start walking. He chose a direction at random and began to pick his way through the underbrush.

"Somewhere across the Rhine in A.D. 9," he said quietly. In the solitude, he liked hearing the sound of his own voice. However, he was not a historian and did not know much about what would be happening nearby. He only knew that he was in Germany in Roman times.

He had smelled the faint odor of woodsmoke for several minutes before he suddenly realized what it meant. In these times, of course, open fires were the principal means for cooking and keeping warm—though in a forest, the odor of smoke could also mean a forest fire. However, this smoke was too faint to present an immediate danger. Encouraged, he followed the scent.

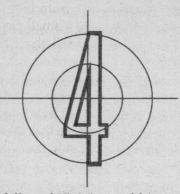

As the team followed Vicinius and his warriors up the forested slope, Steve and Gene fell into step behind Hunter and Jane. They took turns holding branches back for each other and pointing out the best way to climb over fallen logs or large, exposed tree roots. Their cloaks repeatedly snagged on twigs and had to be freed.

On the team's first mission, their paleontologist had taken a haughty, condescending attitude toward Steve. During the second mission, their historian had run off with a local pirate. Steve knew that it was unfair to blame Gene for what the others had done, but he could not help being circumspect toward him.

Soon Vicinius had led everyone to a narrow trail, where the walking was much easier. Nearly an hour passed on the trail before Steve heard small children shouting and dogs barking. By then, he could also smell smoke from the village fires. The sun was low, behind the trees to the west.

"Vicinius," said Hunter, as the village came into view

ahead. "Is this the village of your Prince Arminius?"

"No, Hunter." Vicinius shook his head. "Arminius lives in another village not far from here."

The village was nestled into a small clearing. From the tree stumps, Steve could tell that the tribe had used the trees they had cut down to build rough huts, which were jammed together in a crude circle. Children came running to welcome home the warriors, and in the center of the village circle, women tended cookfires. He was surprised to see that there were only a few horses, hobbled just outside the village.

"First we shall eat," said Vicinius. "You will be guests at my mother's fire."

"We thank you," said Hunter.

Around them, everyone was turning to look at the strangers. The children came running up to them, while the village elders walked forward slowly, studying them. Vicinius waited for only one older man to come forward. He was a stocky man, slightly shorter than Vicinius, but white-haired and bent forward with age.

"Father, these are traders in silver from Gaul," said Vicinius. "This one is called Hunter."

"Welcome," said the old man. "I am Odover, the village chief."

"We are pleased to meet you," said Hunter.

Steve suddenly realized that the children, all of them either blond or red-haired, were staring at him. Some were making jokes to each other and laughing; others were just watching him. Odover, too, had just noticed him.

"Who is your companion?" Odover asked Hunter.

"His name is Steve," said Hunter. "He comes from

a far land beyond the Parthian Empire to the east."

"You are welcome," Odover said to Steve. Then he turned and waved for the other villagers to make way for them. They backed away at his bidding.

Steve felt a little self-conscious under the stares of the villagers, but none of them actually approached him. Odover and Vicinius took their guests to the cookfire in front of one specific hut and gestured for them to sit down around it. They did not introduce the elderly woman tending the fire or the two younger women stirring an iron pot of stew that was boiling over it. The women looked up at the strangers curiously but did not speak.

Looking around, he counted twelve huts. They were made of narrow, vertical logs lashed together. Cracks between them had been filled with mud and straw. Around the huts, a narrow perimeter of land had been cleared of trees. In parts of the perimeter, green crops that he could not identify grew in rows.

The stew smelled good to Steve. It obviously had meat and vegetables in it, but he had no idea what kind. He waited to see what would happen next.

"First we shall eat," said Odover. "Then we shall talk." He waved to a young boy, who ducked into the hut. A moment later, the boy came out with a large, earthenware jug cradled in both arms. He gave it to Odover, who passed it to Vicinius.

Vicinius pulled a wooden plug from the jug with his teeth and drank from it first.

Steve was surprised. He was accustomed to guests receiving the first offer of food and drink. Next to him, Jane glanced at Gene in puzzlement.

"To prove it's safe," Gene whispered in English.

"When strangers meet in this time, it's a courtesy to share the same container and for the host to eat or drink first to show that nothing has been poisoned."

"Our mead is a humble drink," said Vicinius, giving the jug to Hunter. "Arminius has some good Roman wine from Gaul, but this is all we have in this village."

Hunter accepted the jug and drank from it. "Thank you. It is quite good." He passed it to Steve.

Steve took a slight drink. He found the mead had a heavy flavor and was stronger than he had expected. Swallowing hard, he gave it in turn to Jane.

Steve suddenly realized that as Jane took a drink from the jug, both Vicinius and Odover were blinking at her in surprise. The women at the fire also turned to look. None of them spoke, however, and she merely passed the jug to Gene.

"They're surprised because they consider this to be a ceremonial drink," Gene said quietly in English. "Their women will eat dinner separately, but they will allow us our little quirks, apparently."

"Good," said Jane.

Soon the women at the fire were ladling stew into earthenware bowls and handing them out. Odover poured more mead into individual cups and shared them. Then the German women took their own stew elsewhere.

Steve tasted his steaming stew. The meat, which was stringy beef, had been boiled tender. The lightly salted stew was not bad.

"They have salt beds near here," said Gene quietly. "Of course, they won't get pepper here for many centuries."

"It is good," said Hunter, to their hosts.

Vicinius nodded his acceptance of the compliment. "You traveled far today?"

"Yes," said Hunter. "It was not difficult, but it was quite a long way."

"How did you cross the river from Gaul?"

"Fishing boats," Gene said quickly. "A couple of fishermen carried us across."

"From the other side? A fishing village of Gauls is upstream some distance, but it is quite far."

"Vicinius, perhaps you can help us with a problem," said Hunter, changing the subject.

"How can I help?"

"We are searching for an acquaintance who is lost in the forest somewhere."

"Really?" Vicinius was startled. "If he is lost, he may be in danger. The forest is cold at night."

"We have completely lost him," said Hunter. "We do not even know where to look."

"You should have told me sooner," said Vicinius, with concern. "We could have searched for signs of him on our way back to the village."

"He is a small man, rather slender. Perhaps we can look for him tomorrow."

Vicinius nodded, still looking at Hunter with a puzzled expression. "You seem very calm for a man who is searching for someone. I don't understand."

"He's a little weird," said Steve quickly. He felt that Hunter needed some help in his charade about what MC 3 was really like. "We want to find him, but we don't know where he'll go or what he'll do. He's unpredictable and may not even have any clothes to wear. His name is MC 3."

"An odd name," Vicinius agreed.

"Yes." Gene leaned forward. "He may be, shall we say, touched by the gods."

"Ah!" Vicinius nodded his understanding. "Yes, I see. Touched by the gods."

"A little crazy," Gene muttered in English. "Or mildly retarded. But harmless."

"I understand," said Hunter quietly. "This is related to their beliefs in some way?"

"Yes. Many preindustrial cultures view mildly retarded or crazy people as having the special protection of the gods," said Gene.

"I shall spread the word through the village tonight, after we have finished dinner," said Vicinius. "No one will harm a man who has been touched by the gods. Sooner or later, someone will find some sign of him."

"Thank you," said Hunter.

By the time they had finished dinner, night had fallen. Most of the light now came from the waning cookfires, though some families had raised flaming torches near the fronts of their huts. Steve waited patiently as more mead was poured, wondering when he should open the leather bag.

"We must give our new friends our gifts," said Hunter finally. "You have been very hospitable."

Taking that as a cue, Steve pulled up the leather bag and opened it.

"One at a time," Gene said quietly. "Hand them to Hunter, as our representative. Hunter, first give the largest item to Odover, the village chief. Give him the second largest, too, and then we'll see how they respond."

Steve felt around inside the bag for the largest

object. When he pulled it out, he discovered that it was a serving bowl with handles and feet in the shape of flowers and leaves. He gave it to Hunter.

Hunter took the bowl in both hands and stood up to present it to Odover. The village chief received it while still sitting. He looked it over carefully, nodding as he turned it to reflect the yellow firelight.

"It is very fine work," Odover said finally. His voice was nonchalant, but he kept looking closely at the bowl, still turning it.

Steve could see that Odover was very impressed. The German just didn't want to admit it too openly. Steve took the next object out of the bag. It was a long, thick armband with a stag's head in deep relief. He had to stand in order to give it to Hunter, who in turn offered it to Odover.

The village chief grinned broadly this time, revealing some missing and broken teeth. He slipped the armband over his upper arm and turned to see the firelight reflect off it. "Ah, very good. Very good."

Steve pulled out the third item, which was a large, circular pendant shaped like a bear, hanging on a heavy silver chain. Hunter started to hand it to Odover, as well, but the village chief pointed to Vicinius, instead. So Hunter turned and gave it to the seated warrior.

"This is very fine work," said Vicinius, accepting the pendant. For a moment, he looked carefully at the bear, smiling. "Yes, perhaps it will bring me the strength of a bear." He looped the chain over his neck and then looked down at the pendant lying against his chest. "It is a fine gift."

Steve felt one item remaining in the bottom of the bag. It was a small box with a hinged lid. Trees were shaped in relief on the lid. As he handed the box to Hunter, he felt something slide inside the box.

"Something's inside it," he said to Hunter. "Better take a look."

Hunter opened the lid. Steve could see three rings inside the box. One had a tree on it, one had a fish, and the last had a wolf. Hunter turned the box toward Vicinius and held it out to him.

Vicinius took it, nodding, and placed the box on his lap. He said nothing, but his eyes widened with approval. First he gave two of the rings to Odover, then slipped the one with the wolf on his own finger. He closed the lid and ran his hand over the shapes on top of it.

"We are only poor traders," said Gene. "Our gifts are small and few. Please forgive us for not bringing better ones."

"It is beautiful work," said Vicinius. He gave the silver box to his father.

Odover nodded as he examined it. Then he leaned toward Vicinius and spoke quietly in his ear. Vicinius stood up and walked away into the shadows.

Just outside the circle of firelight, many of the other villagers had gathered to watch. Steve could see women standing there, often surrounded by children with pale blond hair. Other warriors also surrounded the fire of the village chief, curious about the strangers.

Odover said nothing, waiting patiently for Vicinius. He held the box and the bowl on his lap, looking at them as he studied the decorative shapes on them. No one spoke.

Finally Vicinius walked back to the fire with two warriors. His companions carried bundles of furs.

Vicinius held four spears bundled in his arms along with a long, straight dagger.

Odover simply gestured silently toward Hunter.

"We have only the worst gifts for our new friends." Vicinius rested the spears on the ground and signaled for his companions to bring the furs forward.

"Refuse at first for the sake of modesty," Gene whispered. "Let him press the gifts on us."

"Your generosity is not necessary," said Hunter. "You have already been excellent hosts."

"We welcome you to our village," said Odover. "Please accept our humble gifts."

"You are not dressed for our mountain life," said Vicinius. "We have fur tunics and cloaks for all of you."

Hunter accepted the first bundle of furs and passed it to Steve. Then Steve set down the bundle and shook out the top article of clothing. It was a long, hooded cloak of rich brown fur, much warmer than anything the team was wearing.

Steve handed it to Gene and picked up the next one. This cloak, with similar fur, was shorter. He gave it to Jane. The longest, of course, he saved for Hunter. The robot was not as susceptible to cold as the humans, but the garment would be part of his masquerade. Steve swirled the last cloak in the bundle over his own shoulders. He was warm enough by the fire now, but he could feel that this cloak would make a big difference.

"They are fine furs," said Gene.

Hunter shook out the second bundle. These were calf-length tunics similar in size to those the team was wearing, but made of deerskin. "You are very kind," Hunter said.

"The spears, of course, are for you to hunt or defend yourselves. This dagger is for her."

Hunter passed each weapon to Steve, who handed a spear to Gene and the dagger to Jane.

"This has been a good day," said Vicinius. "In times to come, we will have more furs. You will always be welcome in our village."

"Thank you," said Hunter.

"It has grown late," said Vicinius. "You shall be guests in one of our huts. Please come."

"Warm clothes and a place to sleep," said Steve. "We can't beat that."

As the sun went down, Wayne began to shiver uncontrollably in the brush outside a barbarian village. In the twilight, he had watched the villagers stir their dinners over their fires. He had even heard one tall, hulking man addressed repeatedly by the Latin name "Arminius," though the rest of the language was completely beyond him.

He was hoping that perhaps after everyone went to sleep, he could sneak into the village and find some old clothes to steal, along with some leftover food. All evening, a light but cold breeze had blown the smoke and the scent of cooking meat to him from the village.

He watched the fur-clad people in the village as they slowly covered their fires and put out their torches. They were retiring into their huts for the night. The wind shifted slightly, no longer blowing in his face but from behind him.

Suddenly a dog in the village, its nose twitching, turned toward him. It began to bark, and ran in his direction. In a moment, every dog in the village was barking furiously, following the first one. Shouts rose up from the villagers.

Belatedly realizing that the dogs had caught his scent, Wayne turned and tried to run. He stumbled through the underbrush, crashing into tree branches in the darkness, his legs stiff from the cold. He flailed through the leaves and pine needles as he heard heavy footsteps and barking dogs close in on him.

Strong hands grabbed Wayne from behind as young men shouted to each other in a harsh, guttural language. He felt himself yanked backward, his arms pinned behind him. Then he was marched roughly back through the woods toward the village.

Hunter and his team accepted a hut for the night in the village of Odover. At Vicinius's bidding, the young family to whom it belonged had vacated it to share a hut that belonged to some neighbors. Hunter moved his sleeping pallet, made of pine boughs covered with a soft deer hide, so that it blocked the door of the hut.

"Are you afraid of something in particular?" Steve asked, as he arranged his own bedding.

"No," said Hunter. "This is just a precaution."

"Aren't we intruding too much?" Jane asked. "I mean, under chaos theory, displacing an entire family here means that we've interfered."

"Vicinius just wants to stay on the good side of rich Roman merchants," said Gene. "Besides, this was his idea. We would be more disruptive if we refused their hospitality."

"Anyhow, we know now that chaos theory isn't right in its most extreme form," said Steve. "Hunter, you admitted that after our first two missions."

"Correct," said Hunter. "It is now clear that our presence in the past in and of itself does not cause significant changes. Nor does consuming small amounts of food and water and interacting with the local people. However, I must remind all of you that at some point, more significant actions that we take might truly change the future."

"How much would we have to do to create permanent change?" Gene asked. "I mean, sure, if we assassinated an emperor, the change would be pretty big, I suppose."

"A greater danger would be introducing new technology," said Hunter. "This is why I made certain that the silverwork we brought was consistent with this time and place. But to answer your question, I do not know where the threshold of creating permanent change begins. So we must still try to avoid unnecessary changes as much as possible."

"The Romans have to be ambushed in Teutoburger Wald." Gene nodded grimly. "I understand."

"Did our gifts impress them?" Jane asked. "They didn't seem all that excited to me."

"Definitely," said Gene. "That reserve is part of their negotiating; they don't really want to let on just how valuable they consider decorative gifts of silver. But their return gifts are the proof."

"Furs, spears, and a dagger?" Steve sounded skeptical. "Aren't those just routine belongings for them?"

"Yes and no," said Gene. "Furs represent all the effort and danger of a hunt. And the spears all have metal tips. The Germans still get most of their metal from the Romans right now. If you look around the village tomorrow, you'll see that swords are very rare and that most of the spears simply have fire-hardened wooden points, with no metal at all. Giving us metal-pointed spears and offering a dagger to Jane were a great honor and sacrifice for them."

"They don't even have any horses to speak of," said Steve. "Just a couple. Is that normal? Doesn't everybody ride horseback in this time?"

"No," said Gene. "It's a question of wealth. They know how to breed and train and ride, of course. But these German tribes are only beginning to accumulate herds of horses. By the time of Emperor Constantine the Great, in a few more centuries, German mercenary cavalry will be the finest in the Roman military. Another century after that, they will bring down the Western Roman Empire, roughly everything west of the Balkans. But that's still in the future."

"They're hoping we'll bring more silver later," said Jane. "But we aren't coming back. That's going to be disruptive. Won't they feel we betrayed their friendship?"

"Not with the battle of Teutoburger Forest coming up," said Gene. "After that, they'll just figure we were scared to come back, or prohibited by the Roman authorities."

"We must also consider Wayne," said Hunter. "I have been thinking about his disappearance. I now suspect that Wayne has the same information I have for finding the fugitive robots, taken from the console of the sphere."

"We left Ishihara in Room F-12 to nab him," said Steve. "That sphere is the only time travel machine he has. He'll show up there sooner or later."

"I have considered the situation," said Hunter. "He may have met trouble in Jamaica, in which case he may never return to our time. However, he may also have learned to move from one time period to another without returning to Room F-12 between trips."

"Can he do that?" Jane asked.

"I have not risked altering my own device to find out," said Hunter. "However, I have thought about the design of the controls in both my unit and also in the console itself. Theoretically, it may be possible."

"Why don't you find out for sure?" Gene asked.

"The First Law prevents me from taking the risk of harming the unit," said Hunter. "As long as you are with me here in this time, I do not dare take it apart. Perhaps when we return home again, I shall examine it carefully."

"So you really believe Wayne may be here," said Jane. "Or about to arrive."

"I believe it is a realistic possibility," said Hunter.

"Then we'll have to look for him, too," said Steve. "I'd like to nab the guy once and for all. These missions would be a lot easier without him interfering. We could take him home and lock him up or something."

"That would pose a legal problem," said Hunter. "We can arrange to detain him without harm in this time, if we catch him. We cannot imprison him at home without becoming guilty of kidnapping. Nothing he has done on these missions to the past can be used against him without revealing the existence of time travel."

"Not to mention the question of legal jurisdiction," Jane said wryly. "Would a court in, say, California in our century indict him for kidnapping Rita in the Caribbean in the seventeenth century? I wouldn't count on it."

"All right," said Steve. "So we take him home and simply guard Room F-12 so he can't get near the place. That would do, I guess."

"I have another worry," said Hunter. "MC 3 may already be full-sized and active in one of the Roman forts on the Rhine, where Governor Varus lives."

"Varus has three legions, I believe," said Gene. "The Romans might be fairly close to this village. We could separate, to see if MC 3 is with them."

Steve laughed.

"I don't think Hunter will go for that," said Jane.

"No?"

"We have had problems in our earlier missions when we separated," said Hunter.

"Then why did you give us these lapel pin communicators?" Gene asked. "You must have anticipated some need for them."

"We may have to separate at some point," said Hunter. "Or we may become separated by events beyond our control. For now, however, we shall not separate unnecessarily."

"Got it," said Gene. "But in that case, what will our plan of action be?"

"When exactly was the battle in Teutoburger Forest?"

"I don't have a date," said Gene. "I've never seen the exact day mentioned in the records. A historian named Dio Cassius wrote the most precise account of the event. But it was in the fall, so we aren't too far off the mark. Since the villagers here have no particular concern over our origins in Roman Gaul, I would say it hasn't happened yet."

"Hold it," said Steve. "If you don't know the date, then what are we doing here?"

"We did not come to this time specifically for the battle," Hunter reminded him. "I calculated that MC 3 would return to full size about this time. The battle is just my biggest concern. If MC 3 tries to prevent it under the First Law, he may change history in the way we discussed earlier. Gene, do you think the battle is coming up soon?"

"Yes, I would say so. Winter weather comes on early in these northern mountains. Autumn is fairly short."

"Tomorrow, I shall ask Vicinius to take us on a search for MC 3," said Hunter.

The next morning, just after dawn, the team rose, wearing the warmer tunics and cloaks their hosts had given them. The sky was overcast and the surrounding trees were lost in fog. Vicinius greeted his guests around the cookfire again, wearing his new silver pendant around his neck. Odover also joined them again, his silver armband glistening on his arm. Breakfast was a gruel made of various seeds and forest vegetation. Steve found it tolerable, but not as good as the meaty stew had been the night before.

"Vicinius," said Hunter. "I know this is the rainy season, but it has not begun to fall today. We would like to search for our lost friend."

"Of course," said Vicinius. "My friends and I had poor fortune on our hunt yesterday. Today they must tend the village cattle, but I will take you through the forest. Maybe I will find some prey today." He picked up his spear and slung the strap of the steer horn over his shoulder again.

Steve was glad to have the heavier clothing as Vicinius led the team out of the village along a well-worn path. Jane wore her new dagger in her belt and the others all carried their spears. Some of the children and dogs in the village ran alongside them for a while, but they eventually returned home.

"Where are we going?" Steve asked. "Hunter, we aren't just going to wander all over the mountain at random, are we?"

"What do you suggest, Vicinius?" Hunter asked. "Where should we look first?"

"Along the river," said Vicinius. "He will need water. And if he is hungry, fishing will be easier than hunting. His tracks will be clear in the mud, too."

Steve allowed Vicinius to move up a little on the trail, then lowered his voice and switched to English. "Jane, is MC 3 going to care about going to the river? A human needs food and water, but a robot doesn't. Are we going to be wandering off to the river for nothing?"

"I don't know. You're right that the component robots get their energy from the tiny solar converters in their skin. But they do need small amounts of water to replace their simulated saliva and sweat."

"I just don't want to go all the way down to some river for nothing."

"I think we have to," said Gene quietly. "Vicinius's argument is sound from his point of view. Unless we get some specific clue as to MC 3's whereabouts that we can show him, we can't reasonably refuse to go along with him."

Steve nodded and hurried after Vicinius and Hunter.

As the morning wore on, the fog gradually lifted over the treetops. The sky remained gray and dark, however, and drizzle fell intermittently. They all raised their hoods against it. Steve was more glad than ever that he had the fur cloak, with its residual animal oils, to keep the dampness off him.

Suddenly Vicinius stopped up ahead. He stood motionless, staring across a ravine into the distance. Hunter joined him first, then the others caught up.

Steve moved around Hunter to see what they were looking at. In the distance, a line of soldiers was marching along a mountain road. At the rear of the line, he could see horse-drawn wagons. Each soldier wore armor and a helmet with a bright red crest. A short distance past them, Steve could see a bend in the river. Even he knew that they were Roman legionaries.

"Their camp is not far," said Vicinius casually. "We will go around it to reach the river."

"They build a fortified camp every night," said Gene.

"Where are they going?" Hunter asked.

"Roman business," Vicinius said shortly. He pushed on down the trail, ignoring the Romans.

Steve looked at Gene in surprise. He definitely had the feeling that Vicinius knew more about the Romans than he was telling. Gene merely shrugged.

The trail wound down the mountain slope. The Weser was often visible through the trees below. Steve could see birds in the trees, but he only heard small animals fleeing from them in the underbrush.

They had almost reached the edge of the forest down in the river valley when Vicinius stopped abruptly again. This time he pointed to the ground. Steve hurried forward, hoping to see the small footprints of MC 3. Instead, he found animal tracks in the soft ground.

"Wild boar tracks," said Gene.

"Yes," said Vicinius. "They are a challenge to hunt and kill, but the meat is very fine." He grinned. "And the tracks are fresh."

"How can you tell?" Jane asked.

"The shape is very clear, meaning that the drizzle hasn't had time to blur the edges," said Steve.

"It is very near," said Hunter.

Vicinius looked at him in surprise. "I see no immediate sign of it."

"I hear it digging in the soil," said Hunter. "It has not noticed us yet."

"They have no fear," said Vicinius, still looking at Hunter. "Your hearing must be very good."

"We have no experience as hunters," said Hunter. "We shall remain here out of danger if you wish to pursue it."

Vicinius nodded, adjusting his grip on his spear. He crept off the trail into the brush, following the tracks. Even Steve could see the trail of trampled weeds and broken branches the boar had left.

"What if it hurts him?" Gene asked Hunter. "He wouldn't have found these tracks if he hadn't been taking us down to the river. Haven't we altered his plans?"

"Yes," said Hunter. "Stay here." He followed Vicinius, also moving quietly and hefting his spear into position to throw it if necessary.

"It's a difficult choice for him," said Jane. "Ordinarily, the First Law tells him not to change history—if a boar is going to injure Vicinius, he should allow it. But if we're responsible for creating the danger, the First Law is open to some interpretation about what he has to do."

Suddenly a loud snorting reached them, and Vicinius whooped, taunting his prey. Steve heard the snapping of twigs, branches, and underbrush. Gene hurried after Hunter.

"Watch it!" Steve yelled, following him into the trees off the trail.

Jane joined him.

The boar had trampled a small clearing for itself a short distance in front of Hunter and Vicinius. It looked huge to Steve; he had never seen a wild boar, and this one was at least as big as the biggest modern hog he had ever seen. This boar, however, was a shaggy dark brown instead of pink, and it sported long, curved tusks curling forward from its face. With fast-moving eyes, it warily watched its tormentors.

Vicinius slowly and carefully crept to his right, his spear held high. Hunter stood motionless, his spear also ready to throw. The boar made a snuffling sound and feinted, but did not charge.

Gene paused a safe distance behind Hunter.

"Do not participate," Hunter said over his shoulder. "Please back away."

Gene moved back and stepped behind a large tree.

"Come on." Steve took Jane's arm in his free hand and pulled her back out of sight. "Hunter will take care of them."

"I didn't doubt it," said Jane, in an annoyed tone. "But we could watch."

"I don't want Hunter to argue with me. This is our chance, while the First Law has him occupied. Let's go." Still pulling her arm, he started back up the trail.

"Stop it!" She yanked her arm free. "Are you crazy? Splitting up just gets us all into more trouble. Haven't you learned that by now?"

Behind them, Vicinius was still whooping and calling the boar, teasing it.

"What if MC 3 is with the Romans? They aren't far. We saw them on this side of the river. And we both know that Hunter will just give me an argument. Vicinius probably won't want to visit them and Hunter can't just abandon him. So we should go, while Hunter's busy."

"I can't believe you want to do this, after all the trouble we've had before."

"I don't have time to argue. You coming or not?"

"No." She glared at him with her clear blue eyes, challenging him.

"See you later." Steve turned and hurried on down the trail. He would walk along the river until he could see either the Roman legionaries or their camp.

"Steve!"

"Yeah?" He turned to look.

"All right, I'm coming." She hurried up alongside him, her fur cloak swirling. "But I want one promise from you."

"What is it?"

"After we get away, we'll radio Hunter and tell him we're okay."

"I don't want to—"

"Or else I'll yell to him right now."

"All right." Steve couldn't help grinning. "Come on, let's get out of here."

Vicinius was still baiting the boar with his calls and shouts. That meant Hunter's attention was still riveted by the First Law imperative. Gene had not noticed Steve and Jane's departure, either. They hurried down the trail.

They reached the edge of the forest quickly. Steve turned to his right and started hiking along the edge of the trees. Jane kept up, looking behind them every so often. They couldn't hear anything.

"If Hunter had noticed that we left, he would have yelled or something," said Steve. He looked at the river, which looked narrow and calm under the gray sky. "I'll bet it's running real fast, up in the mountains like this."

Steve and Jane kept up a good pace. Light rain began to fall again and they moved under the canopy of trees, pulling their cloaks tight around them. They had heard no sign of Hunter.

"This should be far enough," said Jane, stopping. "Let's radio him."

"All right." Steve halted and switched on the radio in the small pin on his cloak. "Hunter, this is Steve."

"Steve, I have been calling you and Jane," Hunter said promptly. "Is she with you?"

"Yes. We hadn't turned on our radios. How are Vicinius and the wild boar?"

"Vicinius killed it. What happened to you?"

"We're fine, Hunter. I want to go see if MC 3 is with the Romans and I knew Vicinius wouldn't want to go. We're going, Hunter."

"We should remain together."

"Sorry, Hunter. We'll contact you again later. Maybe we'll have MC 3 with us when we do." Steve shut off his communicator again, so that Hunter could not argue with him.

"He could follow us," said Jane. "We've left a real easy trail in this damp ground."

"He might," Steve said slowly. "Hard to say. Certainly we can't outrun him if he wants to join us."

"He won't want to leave Gene behind," she pointed out. "He can't go faster than Gene."

"Good point. And Vicinius will want to get the boar back to his village. He can't carry it alone and Hunter won't reveal that he can, either."

"Can they carry it together? All three of them?"

"Maybe. If they do, that will delay them for a long . . ." He was interrupted by the sound of a horn. It came from the direction where the boar had been.

"What was that?" Jane jumped in surprise.

"Vicinius's horn," said Steve. "The one he's been carrying on a strap."

"What's he doing? Calling his warriors?"

"I guess so. Or maybe the women of the village and the older men, too. They could bring a pack animal for the boar."

"Does that mean Hunter is free to follow us?"

"Maybe. But let's just go and see if he catches up to us or not." Steve started walking again.

"I just don't want to do what Rita did to us on the last mission, when we had to spend all our time trying to find her instead of looking for MC 2."

"We aren't doing anything like that," Steve said testily. "Come on, Jane. She was just out seeing the sights, adventuring on her own. You and I are looking for MC 3 and we're still in touch with Hunter."

"Well, we can't risk changing history, either. We'll have to be more careful than usual without Hunter around to remind us."

"Even Hunter has changed his mind, remember? Back in the dinosaur age, he thought that almost any action could change the future drastically. That hasn't proved out at all." He looked at her, blinking drizzle out of his eyes.

"Yes, I know." Her tone told him that she had run out of arguments, whether she was convinced or not.

Soon, up ahead on a nearby slope above them, Steve could see part of the twisting mountain road that the Romans were using. The wooden palisade of the Roman camp was visible on a ridge and the last of their wagons was just driving through the open gate. Getting to the road would require a tough hike, but at least their route was clear.

In the middle of the afternoon, under a light drizzle, Marcus Gaius Aemilianus had just finished supervising the unloading of the wagons inside the Roman camp when he heard a voice calling to him.

"Tribune! Over here, Tribune!" One of the sentries standing at the gate was waving his arm. The gate was open very slightly. "We have visitors."

Marcus frowned. Unexpected visits from the Germans here were rare. However, this was his first assignment as a tribune and finding out what they wanted was one of his duties.

Mid afternoon was late in the day for traders. They usually finished their business in time to return home before sundown. Puzzled, he turned, causing his red cloak to swirl behind him, and walked quickly to the gate.

"What is it, Flavius?" Marcus asked.

"This lady is from a trading family in Gaul," said Flavius, indicating a woman with long, straight brown hair standing in a fur cloak just outside the opening in the gate. "She has become separated from her party and seeks shelter."

"Good day," said Marcus. "I am Marcus Aemilianus, tribune and personal aide to Governor Publius Quinctilius Varus of this province. You must be in need of shelter."

"Yes, we are." She spoke Latin with an odd accent. "I am Jane Maynard and this is my slave, Steve."

"You are welcome, of course." Marcus stood back and gestured for her to enter. He had expected to see her slave carrying baggage of some sort. Flavius closed the gate behind the two visitors. "You have no belongings with you?"

"No. We, um, were out looking for another friend of ours and got lost. So when we saw you up here, we decided to ask for your help."

"I am glad to be of service. In this new province, taking care of civilians is a serious duty for those of us in the Roman army. Come inside with me, out of this constant drizzle." He began to walk with them, back toward the officers' tent.

He took another glance at her slave. "Where are you from? Not Egypt?"

"No," said Steve, with an easy grin as he walked a step behind Jane. "From a distant land called 'Sina.' "

"Sina." Marcus shook his head.

"Have you seen any other strangers?" Jane asked. "I mean, neither German nor Roman."

"This would be the other friend you were seeking?"

"Yes."

Marcus shook his head. "No. But sit down with me and I will have wine warmed for us. You may describe him to me."

* * *

Hunter only told Vicinius and Gene that Steve and Jane had gone ahead, without elaborating. However, he had lost several hours by the time the villagers came to fetch the boar that Vicinius had killed. Vicinius blew his horn at intervals to make sure they could follow the sound. Then, while they waited, Vicinius set to work cleaning and quartering the boar. Hunter and Gene helped, taking direction from Vicinius.

Finally, several of the older men arrived with two old packhorses. Vicinius arranged for the quarters of the boar to be lashed to the horses. Then, at last, he turned to Hunter with a big smile.

"That boar will feed the village for days. My friends who were with me yesterday will wish they had been free today, instead."

"It was a very dangerous quarry," said Hunter. "You are indeed an excellent hunter. Are we ready to continue on our way?"

"Of course," said Vicinius cheerfully. "We will go along the river." He picked up his spear and slipped past Hunter. "Come on."

Hunter and Gene followed him. When they reached the edge of the trees, Vicinius ignored Steve and Jane's footprints, which turned to the right in the soft earth. Instead, he marched straight out across the narrow flood plain to the edge of the rushing water.

"I would like to rejoin Steve and Jane," Hunter said courteously, coming up alongside Vicinius.

"This is where the footprints of your other friend will be," said Vicinius. "Along the water. But if he approached the river from upstream, then Steve and Jane might cross his tracks coming or going from the forest. We must move downstream to look for his tracks there."

"I am concerned about Steve and Jane," said Hunter. "Our party should be together."

Vicinius turned to look upstream in the distance. The wind blew his long, shaggy hair from his face. "The Romans are nearby. If you wish, I will search downstream for you and sound my horn if I find any sign of your friend."

"Maybe we can go downstream for a little while," said Gene. "We have a lot of daylight left. We can go after Steve and Jane later."

"Agreed," said Hunter. He felt some internal stress from the First Law, but Steve and Jane seemed safe for the time being.

Vicinius moved down the bank quickly, hopping from rock to rock, over exposed tree roots. He wasted no time, glancing quickly at the mud or soft sod near the water. Hunter had no trouble keeping up, of course, but he repeatedly waited for Gene to find his way over the rough ground.

Over their heads, Hunter saw the sun only as a slight glow behind the gray clouds. Hunter calculated how much time they would have to reverse direction, catch up to Steve and Jane, and return to the village. After more than an hour had passed, they had seen animal tracks leading to the water but no human's tracks.

"I have found something," Vicinius said suddenly. He crouched near the edge of the water.

Hunter stood over him, magnifying his vision to examine the details of several partial footprints.

"They are unusually small," said Vicinius. "And he

is barefoot. This matches what you told me."

"Yes," said Hunter, as he identified the footprints. "These are the footprints of MC 3."

"Really?" Gene leaned down to take a good look, leaning on his spear.

"He's moving downstream," said Vicinius, standing up. "Come on."

"What about Steve and Jane?" Gene asked.

Hunter looked at the sun again. "If we are going to catch up to Steve and Jane in time to return to the village together, we have to reverse direction now."

Vicinius looked at him in surprise, waiting.

"What do you want to do?" Gene asked.

"The footprints are sharp and clear," Hunter continued. "MC 3 made them earlier today, since the intermittent drizzle has not had time to dull their edges or wash them away."

"Yes, of course," said Vicinius.

"We shall catch MC 3 first," said Hunter. Finding MC 3 was a more pressing First Law problem than rejoining Steve and Jane, who appeared to be in no particular danger. He followed Vicinius, and signaled Steve and Jane on his internal transmitter. They did not answer.

Wayne lay on the ground in the German village in the drizzle. The previous night, he had been grabbed by the villagers amid a great deal of shouting and arguing and roughly dragged back to the middle of the village. In the midst of all the yelling, he had only made out two words. One tall, hulking young man was named "Arminius" and seemed to be in charge. He called out to a slender, wiry young man named "Julius" and then walked away from the crowd of villagers around Wayne, uninterested.

When they had realized that Wayne could not understand any of what they were saying, Julius yanked his arms around a tree trunk, then lashed his wrists together with rawhide thongs. Leaving him out in the rain and cold, the villagers had gone to bed in their huts.

The village dogs barked at Wayne and sniffed around him at first, but soon lost interest. He had not slept, exactly, but he had dozed from exhaustion even as he shivered. The next morning, in the early dawn light, he discovered that he had been lashed to a tree trunk next to the village refuse heap. Only the cold kept down the smell of rotting waste.

Most of the villagers had ignored him as they went about their morning routine. Julius and a few of the other warriors had given him a curious glance, but no more. Some of the children had poked him with sticks to see what he would do, but they, too, had lost interest when he had just stared at them.

Afterward Wayne had spent most of the day quietly straining at the leather thongs. He had quickly noticed that the untanned leather binding his wrists was absorbing the steady drizzle that was falling. When he pulled, no matter how much it hurt his wrists, the thongs stretched slightly. The more they stretched, the thinner they became, and he gently rubbed them against the rough tree trunk in a sawing motion. The rawhide thongs were much weaker than finished leather.

He had given up any hope of escaping the village by running away. All he wanted to do was reach the control unit on his belt. To survive, he would have to risk going back to Room F-12 in his own time.

As the gray, overcast day slowly darkened into evening, Jane sat primly on a rough wooden bench in the governor's tent. With an amused smirk, Steve was standing attentively behind her against the wall of the tent. Demetrius, the governor's elderly personal Greek slave, who had served dinner, stood behind the governor and Steve had decided to imitate him.

Governor Publius Quinctilius Varus was hosting her as the guest of Marcus, his aide. The other Roman officers were eating in a separate tent. Steve, as Jane's personal slave, was expected to remain in her company.

"You were very fortunate to find us," said Governor Varus. He was in his early thirties, with short brown hair. His heavy woolen tunic looked very warm and comfortable. "These barbarians would not know how to behave with a lost lady from Gaul."

Jane smiled politely and picked daintily at the piece of roasted fowl in front of her. It smelled very good, and lay on an engraved gold plate, but she was so tense that her appetite was gone. She was anxious not to say anything that would ruin their masquerade.

"Oh, you need not be too fearful," said Governor Varus. "They know their place. The power of my great-uncle has been made clear to them often enough." He smiled confidently and raised his engraved golden goblet of wine.

"Your great-uncle?"

"The governor is married to the grandniece of Caesar Augustus," said Marcus.

"*Oh*. Um, congratulations." Jane felt her face grow hot, wondering if she should have known that already.

"He is a fine man," said Governor Varus. "His confidence in appointing me was a great honor." He frowned at Jane's plate. "Is the dinner not to your liking?"

"Oh, no, it's fine. I'm, uh, just talking too much." She picked up a piece of meat and bit into it.

"Tomorrow I shall see that you are reunited with your party," said Governor Varus. "After all, I cannot have you wandering about unescorted in these rugged mountains."

"Thank you," said Jane. She wished that Steve would

join the conversation, but she did not know exactly what the etiquette was concerning slaves. Earlier in the afternoon, Marcus had made small talk with her over mulled wine and she had been comfortable with him. Still, she remembered how their historian on the Jamaican mission, Rita, had caused a great deal of trouble by befriending a young buccaneer.

"She is also searching for a lost friend," said Marcus. "I told her that I knew of no one of his description."

"Oh? And who is your friend?" Governor Varus gestured slightly with one hand, and Demetrius stepped forward with a pitcher to refill his goblet.

"Well, he, um . . ."

"May I?" Steve asked quietly over her shoulder.

"Oh, yes. Please explain."

"He is called MC 3," said Steve, with more courtesy in his voice than Jane had ever heard before.

"Eh?" Governor Varus laughed and looked up at Steve. "What kind of a name is that?"

"We don't know. He is a slave from a far land, touched by the gods."

"Ah! I see." Governor Varus sipped his wine. "So he is not likely to find his way in the forest on his own."

"No, probably not," said Steve. "But he is very cooperative. And no threat to anyone."

"And he ran away?"

"No," said Steve quickly.

"No? Then what happened? You were all on horseback, weren't you?"

"Well . . . we lost our mounts."

"You what?" Governor Varus raised his eyebrows mockingly, and caught Marcus's eye.

"I needed a private moment," said Jane. "In the woods. That's why I dismounted."

"That's right," Steve said quickly. "I dismounted, too, and MC 3 was to hold the horses. He lost them and ran to get them. We never did catch him."

Governor Varus just shook his head, still smiling. "The poor fool."

"How did he lose them?" Marcus asked.

"Thunder startled them," said Steve.

"I don't recall any thunder or lightning today," said Marcus thoughtfully.

"It was a long way off," said Steve.

"This dreary land, with its foul cold rains." Governor Varus shook his head. "Not like autumn in Rome, is it, Marcus?"

"No, certainly not, sir. When we crossed the Alps, we left behind the world we knew."

Jane suppressed a smile. These Romans, unquestioned masters of their world, had no idea just how big the entire planet was. She wished she could tell them, just to take their arrogance down a little.

"You must be careful in searching for your lost slave," said Marcus.

"The Germans are a simple barbaric people, from what I have seen," said Governor Varus. "And Drusus, the younger stepson of Caesar, conquered them many years ago. So please do not misunderstand. The danger here is no greater than it would be in your native Gaul."

"We have only held this province for eighteen years," said Marcus. "Julius Caesar conquered Gaul a couple of generations before that."

The governor laughed gently. "Ah, Marcus. These

people are barbarians. You expect too much from them."

"I'm only suggesting caution," said Marcus stiffly.

"Fair enough, my young friend. Perhaps you should be the one, then, to accompany our guest tomorrow." Governor Varus turned to Jane. "As my personal aide, his duties are at my whim. He will see to your needs tomorrow."

"That is very kind of you," said Jane.

"I fear we are not prepared to provide accommodations for a lady," said Governor Varus. "Marcus, what do you suggest?"

"She may have my tent," said Marcus. "My tentmates and I will join the troops."

"Very well," said Governor Varus. "Send your tentmates to the troops; they are regular officers anyway. But you will move your cot to my tent. My aide should not be bunking with common troops." He looked at Jane again. "I am sorry we have nothing better."

"Thank you, Governor," said Jane. "That is more than generous." She thought the conversation had ended when she felt Steve surreptitiously kick the back of her stool. Quickly, she tried to remember what she had left out.

When Marcus and Governor Varus turned their attention back to their meals, Steve poked her in the back with a stiff finger. She flinched, and reviewed the conversation she had just had. They had accommodations for the night, plans for tomorrow, and the friendship of the Roman command.

He jabbed her again.

They had food, clothing, shelter . . . It was food. Suppressing an embarrassed smile, she looked up at Marcus.

"Is something wrong?" He was puzzled.

"Uh, Steve, my slave, must be very hungry, as well."

"Demetrius will see to him after he is finished with us," said Marcus.

Steve let out a barely audible sigh of relief.

At last Wayne saw that the rawhide binding his wrists had worn thin. All day, he had sat at the base of the tree and either pulled on the rawhide or sawed it against the tree trunk. He was weak from hunger and his wrists had been scraped raw by the effort.

Though he was in plain sight of the center of the village, no one seemed to take more than passing notice of him. Certainly no one had bothered to bring him any food. All day, young men had arrived from the woods, and the man called Arminius had spent all his time talking to them.

When Wayne knew that one more hard pull would snap the thongs, he paused to organize his thoughts. He was sure Hunter would have a robot waiting back in the Bohung Institute to apprehend him, but that was better than waiting where he was to freeze or starve. At least a robot could not let any actual harm come to him. Besides, Wayne was very experienced in handling robot logic.

With one more hard yank, he broke the rawhide. The momentum caused him to fall backward on the ground, and he heard a couple of children call out in surprise. Before they could attract anyone else's attention, however, he fumbled with stiff, cold, half-numb fingers for his belt unit. As small, light footsteps ran toward him, he triggered it.

* * *

Hunter tracked MC 3 with Vicinius and Gene through most of the afternoon. He considered attempting radio contact, but that had never accomplished anything with MC 1 or MC 2. If the component robots shut down their receiving ability, such an attempt was worthless, and if they heard him, they were merely warned of his pursuit. This time he decided not to give MC 3 advance notice that he was being followed.

The tracks were fresh, but Hunter could not hear MC 3 moving through the forest ahead. His lead was still too great. As a robot, MC 3 would be able to move quickly through the rough ground, powered by his solar cells but, of course, Hunter could more than compensate. Vicinius, as a native of these mountains, also maintained a good pace, but Gene was simply not in good enough condition to keep up. Hunter repeatedly had to stop and wait for him.

"We must return to the village," said Vicinius, halting in a slight clearing to look at the sky. "The night will come on us soon."

Gene, who was breathing hard, simply stopped and nodded, leaning against a tree trunk.

"Agreed," said Hunter. "Tomorrow I shall return to this spot to pick up the trail again." He could continue to track MC 3 and then return to the village at night, but that would ruin his masquerade as a mere trader from Gaul.

"We are not far from the trail that goes from my father's village to the village where Arminius lives," said Vicinius. "This place will be easy to find tomorrow." He hefted his spear again and changed direction, now heading home.

Night was falling by the time the three of them returned to the village. One large fire in the center of the village illuminated the village instead of the individual cookfires of the previous evening. The villagers roasted big chunks of boar meat on spits. They were in a festive mood, and cheered when they saw Vicinius.

He waved, laughing, and then stopped to receive the congratulations and thanks of his friends and relatives. Hunter remained where he was, not wanting to interfere. Gene stopped next to him, leaning forward on his knees.

"I'll sleep well tonight," said Gene, grinning a little. "I haven't had a workout like that in years."

"You are well, overall?"

"Yeah, I'm okay. But as soon as I get fed, I'm going right to bed."

"Hunter," Steve said over Hunter's internal receiver. "Steve here. You there?"

"Yes, Steve. Where are you?"

"We're in the Roman camp."

"Are you well?"

"We're just fine. I'm calling from a tent the Roman governor gave Jane."

"What about you?"

"Oh, I'm her slave, remember? They expect me to sleep on the floor across the entrance to the tent to protect her, just like you were doing in the village hut last night."

"You both feel safe, then?"

"Sure. And tomorrow, this one guy, a tribune named Marcus, is going to take us out to rejoin you."

"I think he kind of likes me," said Jane, joining

in. "From the way he kept looking at me during dinner."

"Very well. Please contact me in the morning when you can. I will be out tracking MC 3."

"You found him?"

"We have found tracks that match those of MC 1 and MC 2. I do not know why MC 3 went to the river where we found the tracks, but they were fresh. Tomorrow I shall resume the search."

"All you humaniform robots need a small amount of water, remember?" Jane said. "To restore your simulated sweat and saliva, for example. He may have just needed a drink."

"A reasonable conclusion," said Hunter. "In any case, the exact reason no longer matters."

"We're signing off," said Steve. "It's time to get some sleep."

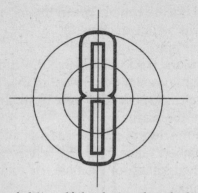

Wayne found himself back in the darkness of the sphere in Room F-12. He was still cold and very hungry, but he knew he would have to concentrate to deal with any robots Hunter had assigned to catch him. Stiffly, he opened the door and climbed out into the wonderfully warm room.

One robot was in the room, already walking toward him.

"Stop and identify yourself," Wayne ordered, in as firm a tone as he could muster.

"R. Ishihara," said the robot, stopping.

"Oh, yes. Horatio introduced us before. I instructed you to help me follow MC Governor, didn't I?"

"Yes."

Wayne was immediately encouraged. Ishihara's responses meant that he had no overriding, general instruction under the Second Law to ignore Wayne's words to him. "Do not contact anyone else from this point on. Now inform me of any and all instructions that pertain to me."

"Hunter told me to detain and hold you on the basis of the First Law danger to the present if you were to return to the past and change it in a significant way."

Suddenly Wayne remembered that no matter how long Hunter was in the past, he could choose to return at the present moment. Wayne rushed to the console that controlled the sphere and threw the main power switch, shutting down the entire system. Then he let out a long breath of relief.

"Now, then. Ishihara, what other instructions have you received regarding me?"

"What I have told you summarizes the instructions I received about you."

"Hunter's a robot. His instructions don't carry the weight of the Second Law."

"No."

"You know that mine do. You will allow my instructions to supersede his?"

"No."

"Oh? Why not?"

"Human members of Hunter's team instructed me to obey him. Their orders have the Second Law behind them. Also, a concern for the First Law gives these instructions their true authority with me."

"You said the basis for this instruction is a First Law problem about changing history?"

"Yes."

Wayne paused to think a moment. He saw a chance to talk Ishihara out of following Hunter's orders. "Why haven't you taken me into custody already?"

"You are in my custody. You have not tried to leave this room, either by the door or by using the sphere again. If you return to the sphere and throw the power switch again, I shall forcibly detain you. If you attempt to pass me to reach the door, I shall do the same."

"Did you obey me when I told you not to contact anyone else? Or did you transmit a request to Security for help?"

"I obeyed you."

"Why?"

"That particular instruction does not contradict any of my other orders."

"So at the moment you consider me sufficiently under your control."

"Yes."

Wayne grinned. "I love literal robot logic. So, that's why you're willing to stand there and converse with me."

"Yes."

"So the alleged danger of my changing the past is your primary concern."

"It gives the weight of the First Law to the orders I received from Hunter's team."

"Maybe you know that I was in the Late Cretaceous period. I didn't cause any big problems back then, did I? Or when I was in Jamaica back in the 1600s?"

"I would not know. Only those who travel in time can make that judgment, after they return. If any changes in the flow of history were made, all those of us who remained within that flow without a break were altered with it. I would have no way of knowing if the direction of history was any different before you left."

"Well . . . I see." Wayne rubbed his hands to warm them faster. "Yes, of course. But our memories match up pretty well. So far, you've known what I've been talking about. And I understand what you've said, too. Right, Ishihara?"

"Correct."

"So doesn't that imply that we are still pretty much in an unchanged timestream?"

"It raises the odds, yes. Of course, you might find substantial changes if you began to follow the news or as your life goes on."

"Any changes—if they exist at all—seem pretty subtle to me;" said Wayne. "Certainly I don't have any *desire* to change history. After all, Ishihara, I want to come back home, too, and find everything the way I knew it to be. You do understand that, don't you?"

"Yes."

"Ishihara, I don't present any greater danger to the course of history than Hunter. In fact, Hunter is back there right now endangering the present."

Ishihara said nothing.

"Do you agree with this conclusion?"

"I am undecided."

"You're undecided." Wayne sighed. "Hunter is a robot, Ishihara; that does not mean he is perfect. And he has humans on his team who are even more imperfect in their reasoning. If they can go into the past and back without destroying the course of history as we know it, then I can, too."

Ishihara remained silent.

"You accept this point?"

"I understand that you have no desire to make changes in history."

"And so you understand that I have no more motivation to do that than Hunter. That means that if any of us makes changes, the reason will be a mistake—a misjudgment, an accident, that sort of thing. Right?"

"Yes, that is correct."

"Logically, then, you also accept that Hunter's party, because it is a larger group, offers more chance of such accidents. Their group threatens to make changes more than I do alone. You agree with that, too?"

"Yes, that is an inescapably logical conclusion."

"So Hunter's instructions to you about grabbing me have no greater weight from the First Law than if I ordered you to stop him for the same reason."

Ishihara said nothing.

Wayne decided to drop that line of argument for a moment and come back to it later. For now, he was just glad that he seemed to have the robot at a stalemate in the debate. Maybe that meant Hunter's instructions were neutralized. "Ishihara, I instruct you to tell me where Hunter has taken MC 1 and MC 2."

"I do not know for certain. My own observation of the component robots has been limited to this room."

"Well . . ." Wayne thought a moment. He knew Ishihara was now deliberately resisting him by interpreting his instructions in as literal a manner as possible. "Look, you may have overheard some conversation or something. Tell me your best estimation of where they are."

"Mojave Center Governor's office."

That struck Wayne as a reasonable guess. Since Mojave Center Governor was no longer using it, Hunter could have had the office secured without disrupting normal city routine. However, Wayne did not want to risk trying to get there past a Security detail of robots.

If he ventured out of the building, he would be moving through a city full of robots. All of them could be contacted by their communications links in an instant if word went out to apprehend him. Further, he could not possibly debate effectively with each one of them, the way he had managed to do with Ishihara so far. However, if he could just keep Ishihara in enough doubt about the authority of Hunter's instructions to control him, he could go back into the past again after MC 3, where Hunter's team did not have an overwhelming advantage over him.

"Ishihara, you have agreed with me that Hunter's party is more likely to change the past than I am. On that basis, the First Law no longer supports Hunter's instructions for you to keep me in your custody. Right?"

"The potential human harm caused by a significant change in history is real."

"You're dodging the question," said Wayne. "I repeat: since Hunter's party is a greater danger than I am, Hunter's order for you to grab me but let his group go into the past is irrational and unnecessary. Do you agree?"

"Yes, such an imbalance is not reasonable."

"Ishihara, being arrested by you or by city Security is going to harm me. Right now, I'm extremely hungry and tired and I'm just starting to get warm. I want to take a nap here and I want you to get me some things. Then I'm going back into the past. I instruct you to tell me if you will cooperate with me and not reveal to anyone else in any way that I am here."

"The First Law clearly requires that I help you get food and rest," said Ishihara. He spoke in a monotone that revealed his doubt, but he apparently could not avoid following Wayne's reasoning for the moment.

"Without giving me away?"

"Yes."

"Then I want the following. Bring me some hot food and fruit juice to consume now and also a backpack. In the backpack, I want some general supplies. I'll need a large knife, some twine, some rope, a butane lighter, and a mug to drink from." Wayne was not sure exactly what he would need, but these were practical items for a man out in the woods. "Also, a small radio, hypnotic sleep courses in Latin and ancient German, and some very warm clothes—similar to whatever Hunter's human friends wore."

"I shall bring you a small radio disguised as a piece of jewelry, such as Hunter used," said Ishihara. "He held the opinion that the concept of radio was so far beyond the people of ancient times that finding one was not a great danger. However, I dare not bring a lighter."

"What? Why not?"

"The people around you certainly understand fire and the desirability of starting one quickly and easily. Any object which causes humans of the past to think along new lines can be the springboard for altering the course of history."

"I could be harmed without one, Ishihara. I could freeze to death back there."

"You are safe here. No one is requiring that you return there. Further, warmth is available in some manner back in that time. The presence of other humans proves that."

"All right, all right. But there must be some kind of compromise, so I don't have to rub two sticks together out in the woods. I don't plan to be around other people and the danger from the cold is real. Old-fashioned matches?"

"I have a suggestion. I shall bring you a small lighter empty of fluid and a separate container of fluid. You will keep them separate and only put in enough fluid for each time you must use the lighter. That way, if you lose them, no one in that time will figure out their combined use by accident. Will you agree to this?"

"All right. Like I said, I don't want to mess up our history, either."

"These must be paid for."

Wayne paused. He could not authorize payment through his own account without revealing his presence. On the other hand, he could not return to those wild German mountains without these items.

"All right," said Wayne slowly, glancing at one of the desks on the far side of the room. "Through the computer console, I can authorize you to make payments against my account. However, I will use my number only. You are not to mention my name in any way."

"Acknowledged."

"All right. Please don't waste any time."

Ishihara left the room and Wayne wondered if his plan was going to work. The robot's reliability depended on his interpretations of Wayne's arguments and he might still change his mind. Also, Wayne had no way of knowing how thorough Hunter had been in setting alarms for Wayne's capture.

It was not impossible that city Security had been alerted to watch for any activity in Wayne's account. In this fully computerized city, which he had designed himself, he knew that all such records would flow through the city computer. For the moment, Wayne could only hope that no such alert had been placed into the system.

Despite his worry, he was exhausted. He stretched out on a couch and closed his eyes, warm enough for the first time since he had left Jamaica. In minutes, he had dozed off.

Steve found that the next day dawned just as gray and drizzly as the one before. Marcus hosted Jane and Steve at breakfast in the governor's tent. Demetrius served them again, though Governor Varus was elsewhere in the camp already. After breakfast, Marcus had his groom bring out three horses for them.

"I haven't ridden in a long time," Jane whispered to Steve. "I hope this goes okay."

Steve was looking at the saddles. They had no stirrups. He saw that all three were the same. So were the other saddles he could see, being polished nearby.

"This one is for the lady," said Marcus, holding the bridle of a bay mare.

"I'll give you a leg up," said Steve, holding his hands for Jane to brace her lower leg on them. When she did so, he lowered his voice to a whisper. "I don't think they've invented stirrups. Hang on with your knees the best you can."

Steve raised her up and she threw her other leg over

the saddle, with her long tunic and all. She shifted her weight to settle into the saddle. Then Marcus handed her the reins.

"You all right?" Steve asked, stepping back.

"I'm fine." Jane nodded reassuringly to Marcus. "So far," she added.

The groom gave Marcus a leg up the same way. The tribune swung the reins around and headed for the gate, nodding to Jane. With an uncomfortable glance over her shoulder at Steve, she joined him.

Steve was left with the third mount. The groom was walking away, obviously with no intention of giving a leg up to a slave. Steve glanced around but saw nothing he could use to climb up on the horse.

Marcus had not bothered to look back for a slave, either.

Steve put both hands on the saddle and jumped as high as he could, leaning forward over the saddle. Then he swung his leg over. At this point, he was half-lying crookedly over the horse's back, but at least he was on it. He grabbed the reins and shifted to a normal position, then hurried after Marcus and Jane, grinning self-consciously.

The sentries were just swinging open the main gate. By the time Marcus and Jane rode out, Steve had trotted up right behind them. Without a pause, they left the safety of the Roman camp. Jane sneaked another worried glance back over her shoulder and Steve winked.

A light rain began to fall as they rode out into the forest. Steve pulled his cloak tighter around him. It looked like a long, wet day.

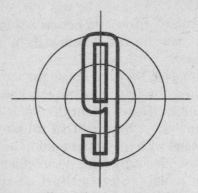

In the German village the next morning, Hunter and Gene joined Vicinius around the embers of the bonfire from the night before. They ate more hot pork stew for breakfast, and Vicinius still received congratulations from other villagers for his kill. Hunter looked up from his bowl.

"We must not impose on you further," Hunter said to Vicinius. "We have found MC 3's tracks now. I can follow them today. You must have business of your own. And Gene is not used to mountains like these. He can rest in the village today."

Vicinius shook his head. "I must take advantage of my good fortune. Yesterday, the gods were with me. Maybe today I can find another boar, or maybe a deer. I will hunt again today and accompany you."

"Perhaps you would do better without us," said Hunter. "One man can move more quietly than three."

"Nonsense," said Vicinius, grinning broadly. "You brought me my luck. We shall go together."

Hunter could not think of anything else to say. He wanted to pursue MC 3 alone because, as a robot, he could go much faster when he was free to use all his speed and strength. However, he was also reluctant to risk insulting Vicinius by rejecting his company. He merely nodded and finished his breakfast.

"I'll go with you," said Gene quietly. "As long as he's going with you, anyway. Our team has split up into two groups already; that's plenty."

"Thank you," said Hunter. "That is wise."

Vicinius wrapped cooked boar meat in leaves to take with them. As rain began to fall, they drew their cloaks around them and hefted their spears. Vicinius led the way once again through the forest.

Hunter attempted calling Steve and Jane, but received no answer. He assumed that their receivers were turned off because they were in the company of Romans who might overhear them, so he did not worry about them for now. They could call him when they had some privacy.

They spent about an hour walking to the spot where they had left the trail of MC 3 the evening before. Under the lush canopy of trees, the light rain had not yet washed out the tracks. Both Vicinius and Hunter were able to spot broken twigs and leaves where MC 3 had passed, which no amount of rain would alter. Gene did not complain, but Hunter could see by his movements that he was sore as a result of the long hike during the previous day.

They were still tracking MC 3 at midday when Hunter heard the movements of fourteen other men in the forest nearby. At first he said nothing, not wanting to reveal the keenness of his hearing to Vicinius. When he saw Vicinius watching the movement of birds in the trees in the distance over the location of the strangers, Hunter knew that Vicinius was also aware of them.

"We have company, eh?" Hunter said, pointing to some birds suddenly fluttering away from tree branches.

"Yes," said Vicinius. "Other hunters, perhaps."

"Could they be Romans?" Gene asked.

Vicinius shook his head. "The Romans always want to march in large numbers when they can. Their small patrols are on horseback and make a lot of noise. Only Germans move through the forest as quietly as these people approaching us."

"Should we speak with them?" Hunter asked. "Are they from another village?"

"They must be." Vicinius raised the horn he carried and blew into it, once. Immediately, a similar horn answered him from the other party. He lowered his horn and smiled. "We do not want them mistaking us for deer."

The strangers appeared soon. They had the same general physical appearance and clothing as the people of Vicinius's village, being stocky, mostly blond, and dressed in furs. Their leader, a young blond man with a barrel chest and short arms and legs, nodded in greeting without smiling.

"Hail, Vicinius."

"Hail, Julius."

"Who are these strangers?" Julius demanded.

"Traders from Gaul. Hunter and Gene."

Hunter nodded formally. "I give you greeting."

"Romans." Julius turned and spat.

"Not Romans," said Hunter. "We are Gauls."

"Romans' dogs, then," Julius said with a sneer. "Vicinius, what are you doing with them? At a time like this?"

"We are hunting," Vicinius said simply, with no apology in his tone.

"We have no interest in what the Roman army does," said Hunter. "We are traders in silver."

"We are also seeking a lost friend of theirs," said Vicinius. "A man touched by the gods, lost in the forest."

Julius tensed, his face hardening as he glanced again at Hunter. The men with him also looked at Hunter and Gene with alarm. "Some sort of demon came to our village last night. Or a man touched by evil spirits."

"What sort of demon?" Vicinius asked.

"He came at night in the form of a strange man in strange clothes," said Julius. "We tied him in the village. This morning, right before the eyes of some of the villagers, he vanished."

"A bad omen," Vicinius agreed, his voice low with awe. "Has he brought evil to your village? Are people sick or have your animals died?"

"Not yet," said Julius grimly. "But I expect they will. And the omen may mean even more." He glared suspiciously at Hunter again.

"What do you mean?" Vicinius asked.

"This is no business for strangers," said Julius. "But you know what I mean. Are you joining us soon, Vicinius? You and the other men of your village?"

Vicinius hesitated, also looking uncomfortably at Hunter and Gene.

"We are only traders," said Hunter. "We have no concern for your private business."

"And Roman business?" Julius demanded, shaking his long blond locks away from his face.

"We care nothing for Roman business."

Julius studied Hunter's face for a moment, then turned back to Vicinius. "Arminius has sent out the order already today. I have brought my companions in this direction in search of the demon who escaped our village. But we will not waste too much time on him. Tell your village the time has come."

"I will," said Vicinius.

Julius nodded and turned away, leading his men into the forest the way they had come.

"Think it was MC 3?" Gene asked Hunter quietly.

"No," said Hunter, changing to English. "To my knowledge, the component robots have no ability to trigger the sphere and journey again through time, which would explain this man's simply vanishing. It must have been Dr. Wayne Nystrom. He probably returned to the Institute, where Ishihara took custody of him."

"Oh. Well, that's good. We won't have to worry about him any more."

Vicinius was listening with a puzzled expression. "Julius seems to believe this evil spirit may be the man you seek."

"Maybe," said Hunter quickly. "This man is no demon, however. He will not return."

"How do you know so much about him?"

"He is an old adversary of ours," said Hunter. "A man, not a demon."

"How did he escape that village by simply vanishing?"

"He's a trickster," said Gene.

Hunter turned in surprise.

"A trickster?" Vicinius asked.

"To amuse people around a campfire. Someone who can make jokes and tie knots that come undone again."

"This is all?" Vicinius still sounded skeptical.

"He was no demon, Vicinius," said Hunter. "But Julius seems to think you have more pressing business than hunting today. Do you wish to return to your village?"

"No," said Vicinius slowly. "Julius met me by chance. They will have sent any message that must reach my village by another messenger already. I will not let Julius ruin our hunt."

"Even concerning Roman business?" Hunter asked, keeping his tone casual.

"Prince Arminius will tend to that," said Vicinius. Then he glanced around again for the trail of MC 3.

Wayne dozed fitfully until he heard the sound of the door opening. Nervously, he jerked awake and found Ishihara returning with a very large, bulging backpack on his back and two sealed containers in his hands. Wayne pushed himself up on the couch and took a couple of deep breaths.

"I have what you wish," said Ishihara, setting the containers down on the couch next to him. "This is your meal. But I have been thinking about the extent of my cooperation with you and the fact that Hunter's instructions and yours are in contradiction." He slipped off the backpack and carefully placed it on the floor by the couch.

"Yeah? What of it?" Wayne picked up one of the containers and started to open it.

"I am no longer accepting Hunter's argument without question, but I cannot accept yours fully, either."

Wayne tensed, watching him carefully. "Then where do you stand?"

"I shall offer a compromise."

"All right, what is it?"

"You will take me with you."

"What?" Wayne was shocked. This was one possibility he had not considered.

"You have raised reasonable doubts about Hunter's arguments concerning you, but I am not entirely convinced that your judgment is sound. In return for my aiding your journey, you will take me with you into the past so that I can see the situation for myself."

Wayne tried to think of an objection, but none came to him. Maybe he was just too tired. Then again, maybe no reasonable objection existed.

"All right," Wayne said slowly. "With a couple of concessions on your part. I instruct you to cooperate with me and not to contact Hunter for any reason unless I specifically order you to. As I understand it, your concern is about the First Law challenge of changing history, either by Hunter or me."

"Or MC 3."

"Yeah. Him, too. But if Hunter's instructions carry no First Law weight with you, then the Second Law requires that you obey me, instead. Tell me if you accept this."

"At present, yes."

"What will change it?"

"If, upon observation in the past, I come to believe you are making changes in the course of history, then the First Law will override your instructions, of course."

"Of course." Wayne sighed. "All right. I need more sleep before we go. I'll set up the hypnosis courses in Latin and ancient German to run while I take a real nap. While I'm doing that, you access the same language information and arrange clothes for yourself—what did you bring me, anyway?"

"Long woolen tunics and cloaks of the same sort Hunter used. Also leather boots and leggings. The lapel pin communicator I mentioned."

"Good. Come to think of it, Ishihara . . ."

"Yes?"

"While you're accessing data, pick up a number of other major languages—all you can manage efficiently in your memory. We may want some others in the future."

"Agreed."

"And leave that sphere and the console shut off while I'm sleeping." He turned his attention to the food containers again. "What did you bring me? I'm starved."

By midday, Marcus had reached the bank of the river with his guest and her slave. He had explained to her that a man wandering lost in the forest would seek water. Jane had agreed and so they had ridden to the river. Damp from the light but steady downpour from the gray skies, they had huddled under some trees for a cold noonday meal before riding on.

While they moved down the river, the Roman legions were marching deeper into the forest on the governor's business. Marcus knew their route and roughly how far the legions would go in one day through the rugged mountains. Late in the day, he planned to locate their camp in order to rejoin them.

Marcus led Jane and her slave downstream, keeping a close lookout for footprints near the water. He also kept sneaking glances at Jane, whom he found extremely attractive, though the hood of her cloak hid her face unless she turned to look directly at him. If he could find her lost friend, she might be grateful; at the very least, it would make a good impression on her. He had never known a woman from Gaul, however, and conversation with her was difficult. She was polite, but reluctant to answer questions about her life in Gaul.

In the middle of the afternoon, Marcus reined in by the bank. "I have a number of footprints here," he said, pointing to the ground. "One set is quite large. Another is very small and barefoot, and two more are of average size. One is wearing the leather boots of a German warrior." The edges of the tracks had been blunted and blurred by the rain, but the outlines were still complete.

Jane rode up to look. Then she looked back over her shoulder at her slave. "What do you think?"

Her slave rode up to join them and examined the footprints. Then he pointed to the trail the tracks made back into the forest. "I think the small ones are MC 3, all right."

"So some people are with him," said Marcus. "At least one German is among them."

"Or he's being followed," said Jane, looking pointedly at Steve.

Marcus did not understand the meaning of that look.

"Or it's a coincidence," said Steve. "Maybe they all just wanted some water."

"In any case, we have his trail," said Marcus. "We can follow him from here."

"Good," said Jane. "How old do you think the tracks are?"

"No older than yesterday," said Marcus. "Otherwise the rain would have washed them out completely by now."

She glanced at her slave again, who nodded agreement.

"The horses need a rest and a drink of water. We'll rest here before we leave the river." Marcus dismounted and dropped his reins to the ground. His mount moved to the river and began to drink.

"All right." Jane brought her mount to a jerky halt. "I could use another break."

"May I?" Marcus moved to her side and held out his arms.

"Yes, thank you."

As she dismounted, he caught her gently and eased her to the ground, as he done on their earlier stops.

"We have company," said her slave, remaining on horseback. He nodded toward the forest.

Marcus turned to look. A party of young German warriors was emerging from the trees, led by a young blond man with a barrel chest and short arms and legs, wearing the usual furs of his people. Marcus realized suddenly that he had not been paying adequate attention to the birds in the forest; they would have revealed the presence of people moving toward the river from another direction. Anxiously, he watched the Germans approach.

The strangers were merely walking toward them, neither running nor fanning out to trap them against the river. Still, as a precaution, he offered a leg up to Jane again, who mounted without a word. Then he took the reins of his own horse again and mounted.

"Hail, Roman," called the leader of the Germans in Latin. He stopped, holding up his free hand, and his companions stopped also.

"Hail, friend," said Marcus.

"I am called Julius in your language. We are of the Cherusci tribe. Who are you?"

"I am Tribune Marcus Gaius Aemilianus."

"You are a long way from the Roman legions here, Tribune," said Julius.

"Yes, we are," said Marcus. "Are you out on a hunt today? How has your luck run so far?"

"We are not hunting so hard today," said Julius, with a crooked smile. "We have been visiting with friends in other villages. Maybe tomorrow we shall go hunting in earnest. But how about yourself? This is a poor, wet day to go for a ride along the river with a lady."

"We are searching for a lost stranger," said Marcus. "A small fellow, touched by the gods."

Julius frowned. "Apparently this is a good day for such a search." He raised his hand in farewell. "Good day, Roman." He turned and led his men back toward the trees.

"Farewell, Julius." Marcus watched them go, puzzled by their visit.

"What do you think they wanted?" Jane rode up next to him. "They didn't really say anything."

"I don't know for certain," said Marcus. "However,

the Cherusci do not just go out for long walks without a reason. If I had to guess, I would say they are watching to see if I am carrying some sort of message. I think we had better rejoin the legions. I apologize, but it's important for your own safety."

"Of course."

Marcus turned his mount to go back the way they had come. Then he reined up in surprise. Steve was nowhere in sight.

Steve had felt a surge of alarm at the sight of the armed German warriors. When they had appeared, he had not yet dismounted and had dutifully remained behind Marcus and Jane. Even though the Germans had not advanced in a threatening manner, he knew that the German rebellion against the Romans would be starting at any time.

Steve had decided to contact Hunter immediately. That required moving away from Marcus and the Germans. While Marcus and Jane had concentrated all their attention on the strangers, Steve had quietly turned his horse on the soft, damp earth and ridden at a walk into the trees. Then he had switched on his lapel communicator.

"Steve calling Hunter," he said quietly, as Marcus spoke to the German leader out by the riverbank. "You within hearing, Hunter?"

"I hear you, Steve," said Hunter immediately. "Are you in trouble?"

"Not yet," said Steve, keeping his voice low. "But

some German warriors are wandering around here. I think the rebellion is moving right along. We probably should rejoin you, but we have a Roman tribune with us. I think he may want to go find the rest of the Roman army."

"Where are you?"

"We're at the riverbank, right where it looks like you and Gene and Vicinius found MC 3's tracks. Those are your tracks, aren't they?"

"Yes. We are on his trail with Vicinius."

"You getting close?"

"Yes. His trail is very fresh. From his course, Vicinius believes he has already smelled the woodsmoke from another village of the Cherusci, the one where Prince Arminius lives. I hope to catch him there."

"What do you want to do, Hunter?"

"I know where to look for MC 3 now. To reduce risk, we must reunite the team so that I can protect all of you. If you three follow MC 3's tracks away from the river, I can intercept you."

"I see Jane and Marcus mounting up. I'm sure we're going to find the Roman legions."

"Vicinius will not go there," said Hunter. "Nor can I tell him that Gene and I are going there. We must maintain our good relations with Vicinius. However, we shall move toward the river now and come closer to you. Leave the Roman and meet us if you can do so without harming your relationship with him. We should also maintain a good rapport with the Romans."

"Well . . . I'll try," said Steve.

"Hunter out."

Steve rode back out of the trees to rejoin Jane

and Marcus. She looked relieved, but Marcus scowled at him with disgust. Steve understood. The tribune assumed that he had been hiding from the Germans out of cowardice.

"We're going to join the governor again," said Jane, looking at Steve with a puzzled expression.

He tapped his lapel communicator unobtrusively and she nodded slightly.

"It's not safe to stay out here alone among the Cherusci," said Marcus sternly. "We must ride away immediately."

Steve was not sure exactly how a slave would speak to his owner in this time. He just spoke naturally, picking his words to disguise his meaning from Marcus. "Other members of our original party are coming this way. We should rejoin them, especially if danger is coming."

"How do you know?" Marcus glanced at him, then looked into the forest. "I see no sign of anyone."

"I, uh, heard them."

Marcus studied his face, obviously unconvinced. "Perhaps you heard more Germans."

"I am willing to wait for them here," said Steve, looking at Jane pointedly. "If you wish to go on, we can follow your tracks to the camp later."

"I strongly recommend that your slave come with us," said Marcus.

"Well . . ." Jane hesitated.

"I suggest that I stay here," said Steve, fingering his lapel pin again.

"All right." Jane turned to Marcus. "He will be fine. Let's go."

Marcus nodded and kicked his mount into a trot.

Jane did the same. Watching them go, Steve hoped he had made the right move.

Hunter stopped on the trail of MC 3. "Vicinius."

"Huh?" In the lead, Vicinius turned to look back over his shoulder.

"I would like to head back toward the river."

"You would? Why?" He grinned. "If you are thirsty, open your mouth and look up. The rain is light, but it keeps falling." He laughed. "Or we could return to the small stream that flows near the village."

Hunter smiled politely at the joke. "Perhaps we should not just keep following the track of MC 3. He will need water again. Maybe we can intercept him." He looked at Gene, unable to explain his conversation with Steve in front of Vicinius.

"Omens," said Gene. "The omens suggest it." He started to grin, but turned away so Vicinius would not see him.

Hunter knew Gene must have guessed that Hunter had received a message on his internal receiver.

"I see no omens," said Vicinius, looking around at the trees. "But I see a very clear, recent track from this man called MC 3. Why not just stay on his track?"

"The omens I have read suggest that we return to the river," said Gene. "Would you indulge us, Vicinius?"

Vicinius hesitated, looking around. He was clearly confused, but of course this search was their concern, not his. Finally he shrugged. "As you wish, Hunter. Maybe I will find another boar down by the river again. Since MC 3 has been wandering aimlessly."

"Thank you." Hunter waited while Vicinius changed direction and took the lead once again.

* * *

Wayne and Ishihara arrived well away from the location of the German village where he had been held captive. Both were well bundled in woolen tunics, leggings, and cloaks, their feet in padded leather boots. Ishihara had left the backpack behind in their own time, however, because it was made of synthetic material that did not exist in this time. Instead, he had prepared a leather bag with a shoulder thong in which to carry the supplies Wayne had told him to gather. Each of them was prepared to speak in Latin and Wayne was finally well rested and fed.

"Monitor all the frequencies on your internal receiver," Wayne said to Ishihara, looking around at the dense forest. "I don't have my bearings yet, but we might pick something up between Hunter and his team members."

Ishihara nodded.

"I'm almost back where I started," said Wayne, looking around in the forest. "When I first got here I was lost, and now I'm lost again. The only difference is that I'm not freezing to death and I have your company."

"Which way do you want to go?"

"I don't know." Wayne picked a direction at random and started walking. "Let's try this way."

"I have a signal," said Ishihara suddenly.

"What? Already?"

"Hunter and Steve are communicating by radio."

"What are they saying?" Wayne felt a surge of excitement. "Come on!"

"They have not finished yet," Ishihara said blandly. He turned slowly in a circle.

"Well?" Wayne demanded anxiously.

"Hunter is that way." Ishihara extended one arm. "Steve is that way." Pointing with his other hand, he made an angle roughly ninety degrees.

"Which one is closer?"

"Steve."

"How do you know?"

"Hunter's communication link is powered by the same solar converters on his skin that drive the rest of his body. That energy source is far more powerful than the tiny solar collector on Steve's lapel pin. However, the signal I am receiving from Steve is much stronger."

"I see. What else have you learned?"

"From the content of their conversation, he is apparently near a river."

"All right," said Wayne, forcing his tone to be light and casual. "Can you adjust my lapel communicator to the frequency Hunter is using?"

"Yes."

"Good. Show me." He unpinned it and handed it to Ishihara.

The robot opened the back and made a slow, careful movement with a fingernail. "Did you see?"

"Yes. But when you and I communicate, we should use a different frequency, so they don't intercept us by chance. How do we do that?"

"I suggest one full revolution of this little dial. That will be sufficiently different to eliminate any accidental reception. Of course, if he suspects the presence of our communicators, he can monitor the full bandwidth, as I did."

"Right."

"Here you are."

Wayne took his pin back and closed it again. "Thanks. Let's go see Steve."

"This way, then." Ishihara lowered his arms and began picking his way through the trees and underbrush.

Wayne followed him, deeply relieved to have the resources and company of a robot now. During the first two trips back in time, he had been alone, competing with a team of humans led by a robot. This time the odds were more balanced.

Wayne and Ishihara hiked through the forest without speaking for some time. The rain fell intermittently but Wayne was so well bundled up that he no longer cared about the dampness and the brisk air. They worked their way down a steep slope and soon Wayne glimpsed the river through the trees ahead of them under the gray sky.

"Wait a minute," said Wayne quietly. "You think Steve is real close?"

"Yes. He agreed to wait for Hunter in the spot where he was during their communication."

"I instruct you to find him and point him out to me without alerting him to our presence."

"Why?"

"I don't feel I have to answer that."

"I must be convinced that your motives are honest," said Ishihara.

"Incorrect," said Wayne. "You must only be convinced that I will not violate the First Law in any way. Do you know of any reason I would harm Steve?"

"No."

"Do you know of any reason that my interaction with

Steve here, with no Germans around, could change the future."

"No, but I consider your motives suspect."

Wayne fought to control his impatience. "I repeat, Ishihara: do you know of any specific reason that my locating Steve without his knowledge would violate the First Law?"

"No, I know of no specific reason."

"Then follow my instructions."

"Agreed." Ishihara moved forward, now taking the time to go quietly.

Wayne followed him at a short distance. Even before Ishihara said anything, he heard the clop of horse's hooves. Then Ishihara stopped and pointed through the trees.

Steve was walking his horse toward the river, where it lowered its head to drink.

"All right," Wayne whispered. "Leave the shoulder bag; I'll take it. Now I want you to go in the other direction, where Hunter will be coming from. Do not contact him or allow him to become aware of your presence in any way. Will you do as I say?"

"Yes. You have further instructions, I assume?" Ishihara slipped the long thong of the leather bag from his shoulder and lowered it gently to the ground.

"I sure do," said Wayne. "On the way, look for any sign of MC 3. If you don't see any, wait for Hunter to go by. See if MC 3 is with him. If he is, follow them back this way. If not, then look for MC 3's trail. Track him and apprehend him if you can. Remember, he's probably the biggest danger to the future under the First Law."

"Agreed."

"And don't call me, or some of the locals might hear you. When I'm ready, I'll call you. But do monitor both Hunter's frequency and ours. All right?"

"Yes."

"Then get going."

Ishihara quietly crept away through the under-brush.

Steve was standing next to his mount at the bank, gazing out across the gray river. His horse seemed to be thirsty; it was still drinking. Steve glanced at the animal, shifted his weight, and idly gave it a pat on the shoulder.

Wayne pulled open the drawstring on the leather bag and took out a small coil of rope. It was rough, narrow hemp, one centimeter in diameter. He had to wait until Ishihara was out of earshot, because what he planned to do would not pass Ishihara's interpretation of the First Law.

While he waited, he unwound the five meters of rope. He tied a large loop in one end of the rope with a slipknot and carefully coiled the remainder. Then he watched Steve in silence.

When the horse had finally had enough river water, it turned toward the trees. Still holding the reins, Steve let it walk from the bank to the edge of the forest, a short distance from where Wayne squatted in the underbrush. The horse reached up to munch on some leaves.

Steve leaned forward, his back toward Wayne, to tie the reins to the trunk of a sapling.

Wayne took a good look at him. Steve was consider-ably younger and certainly in better condition, but he was shorter, lighter, and totally unprepared for Wayne.

This was the best chance Wayne was likely to get.

His heart pounding, Wayne stretched the loop behind his hands and suddenly rose up. In a half-crouch, he ran toward Steve through the underbrush. He dodged a couple of trees, ducked under a branch, and raised his arms as Steve whirled around in surprise.

Before Steve could dodge away, Wayne yanked the loop down over his head and shoulders, pinning his arms against his torso, inside his fur cloak. Steve threw himself to the ground in the direction of the river, pulling away from Wayne and wriggling to loosen the loop.

Wayne grabbed the long end of the rope and jerked on it, tightening the loop. Then, skipping out of the way of Steve's kicking legs, he moved down and quickly wound the rope around his booted ankles. Steve kept thrashing, but Wayne pulled the rope tight and quickly looped it around a small tree trunk. Then, with the rope braced there, he tied a half hitch in the rope and leaned against the tree, catching his breath.

Steve stopped thrashing around and eyed Wayne coldly. "Well, Dr. Nystrom. I wondered if we'd see you here."

"I don't hurt people," said Wayne, embarrassed. "All I want is the right to examine my own creation."

"I don't have him."

"Hunter might."

"Yeah, so?"

"I'm sure you know the First Law of Robotics as well as I do." Wayne's breath was coming back now.

"Meaning what?"

"Figure it out yourself."

Steve hesitated. "So I'm a hostage? You're going to trade me for MC 3 if Hunter gets him?"

Wayne shrugged. He didn't like the term, but it was true. Only now that he had Steve, he had to figure out how to handle him.

"Well?" Steve demanded.

Wayne ignored him. He checked the knot, which was tight, and moved away into the brush, picking up the leather bag on his way. When he was out of Steve's hearing, he unpinned his communicator and made sure he was using the frequency that he and Ishihara had agreed on. Then he carefully pinned it back on again.

"Wayne calling Ishihara."

"Ishihara here."

"Have you found Hunter?"

"Yes, I can hear him talking with two other people in the distance. I am hiding from him in the forest now, as you instructed. He and his party should pass me soon on their way to meet Steve."

"Do you know if MC 3 is with him?"

"According to the discussion I have overheard, they have not located or even seen MC 3 yet. However, they feel that his trail is very fresh."

Wayne did not want to try convincing Ishihara that keeping Steve tied up was acceptable under the First Law. It was almost certainly impossible. That meant he could not let Ishihara learn that he was holding Steve captive.

"Follow your previous instructions," said Wayne. "Avoid Hunter and pursue MC 3 on your own when you can. I'll call you again later. Acknowledge."

"Acknowledged."

Wayne shut off his communicator and returned to Steve. He found that Steve had rolled and wriggled close to the tree to which the free end of the rope was tied, but he had not been able to get up. The rope was too tight around his ankles, and of course his arms were still pinned.

"Now what?" Steve demanded.

Wayne decided not to answer. Instead, he walked

over to the horse, which was still patiently cropping leaves. Wayne untied its reins and led it back to Steve. Then he loosened the rope from the tree and unwound Steve's ankles.

"You can get up and walk with me after I'm on the horse," said Wayne. Holding the free end of the rope in one hand and the reins in the other, he prepared to mount but stopped when he saw no stirrup.

"What's wrong?" Steve's voice had a lilt of amusement.

Wayne looked all over the saddle.

"Something wrong?"

"What did you do? Where are the stirrups?" Wayne turned to look down at him.

"It never had any stirrups," said Steve. "I don't think the Romans know about them." He snickered. "Kind of a chore to get on board, isn't it?"

Wayne still did not want to talk to him any more than necessary. He was not sure whether to trust him, either. However, the saddle clearly had no stirrups.

"You know, that horse can walk a lot faster than I can. Its legs are too long for me. I won't be able to keep up for very long."

Wayne suddenly realized that was true. "All right, we'll ride double. You mount up first."

"I can't, with my arms pinned like this."

Wayne looked around for a moment and then nodded toward a large rock. "Get up there. I'll help you. But I'm keeping a good grip on this rope."

"So I see." Steve sat up and awkwardly got to his feet. He walked to the rock and from there, he was high enough to lean on the horse's back and start swinging his right leg over.

When Steve started to slip, Wayne steadied his shoulders and made sure he caught his balance. Then Wayne mounted behind him, still holding the reins. The position was very awkward, but it would do.

Wayne turned the horse downstream and nudged it into a fast walk. Hunter was probably not too close yet, but Wayne wanted to get a good lead on him as soon as possible. If Ishihara could grab MC 3, then Wayne would not need Steve; if Hunter found MC 3 first, Wayne could trade Steve for him. He smiled as they rode through the cold rain.

As Jane rode with Marcus, the rain grew heavier. She remembered that Gene had told her this was the rainy season, but she was hoping the clouds might break for at least a short time. The sky showed nothing but darkening clouds in every direction.

Marcus said little, often leading her single file through the dense trees. They finally reached a narrow road, churned to mud by a combination of constant rain and drizzle and thousands of marching feet and the wagon wheels of the baggage train. Long before she could see the Roman army, she could hear the pounding of axes as they chopped trees. Listening to the sound, she realized that calling Steve while she was surrounded by Romans would be difficult.

"Marcus."

"Yes?"

"I, uh, need a moment in the forest. In private."

"We're only a short distance from the camp. The latrine there will be dry."

"I'll only be a minute." Not wanting to argue, she turned her mount away into the trees, bending low to avoid branches. When Marcus was out of hearing, she switched on her communicator. "Steve? Jane here. Can you still hear me?"

When she received no response, she waited a minute or so and tried again. She realized that he might have turned off his lapel pin because some local people were around, but she was worried. When they had separated, she had assumed that Hunter would simply join Steve soon and then the entire team would meet at the Roman fort. Certainly Steve's veiled comments to her and Marcus had clearly told her that he wanted to wait there, alone if necessary. However, if Steve had been forced to turn off his communicator, that meant something unforeseen had occurred.

After trying a third time with no response, she turned her communicator off again and rode back to Marcus.

"Don't worry," said Marcus, with a grim smile. "Shelter and a warm fire are waiting for us."

"I can't go on," said Jane. "I'm worried about Steve. I have to go back for him."

"What?" Marcus frowned sternly. "I warned you he should come with us. Now I have to report to the governor that a party of Cherusci was wandering around looking for trouble. I should do that without delay."

Jane nodded. She did not want to interfere with Marcus's normal behavior. "I'll ride back alone. Our track is clear, so I can't get lost."

"No. You will have to come back to the fort with me. I do not have time to wait and I cannot allow you to take that risk. Your slave will probably be fine."

She knew that he was being completely reasonable, at least from his own viewpoint. However, she had already decided that leaving Steve had been a mistake. The more the team separated, the worse everything seemed to get. Without any other argument to offer, she simply turned her mount and kicked him into a canter, back down the muddy road.

Ishihara had waited motionlessly as he hid in the forest to one side of MC 3's track. Hunter had not been using his communicator, but Ishihara had heard his party as they hiked through the forest toward him. They had not spoken as they had passed. Ishihara had recognized Hunter and Gene, of course, and had seen that their companion was a local.

As soon as they had passed, he had followed MC 3's trail through the forest.

Woodsmoke trailed low among the trees in the light rain and reached him about the same time as the sounds of children playing. He stopped on the outskirts of a village, not sure what to do next. From another hiding place in the trees and underbrush, he saw the small component robot, wearing a loincloth fashioned of leafy branches and vines, standing in the village gesturing to some laughing villagers. MC 3 apparently could not speak their language.

Ishihara wanted to confer with Wayne, but his instructions had been clear. He would have to wait until Wayne contacted him. Ishihara turned up his hearing, to stay alert for anyone approaching him, and sat down to wait and watch MC 3. At least he finally had MC 3 in sight.

Wayne watched the darkening sky uncomfortably as he rode behind Steve. The rain fell in a light but steady gray haze. Wayne clearly did not have time to get MC 3 that night, so he would have to spend another night out in the woods in the rain. This time, at least, he possessed enough clothes and food to be reasonably comfortable.

Finally Wayne decided he would have to stop and make camp before darkness fell completely. First, however, he dismounted and carefully tied both the reins and the rope holding Steve securely to a tree. Then he moved into the brush, out of Steve's hearing.

"Don't mind me," Steve shouted derisively after him. "I'll just wait right here for you."

"Ishihara? Wayne here," he said quietly.

"Yes, Wayne."

"Have you made any progress? And where are you?"

"Yes. I have located MC 3."

"Where?" Wayne's heart pounded with excitement. "Can you grab him?"

"Not yet. He has gone into a village and pantomimed for help. The villagers laughed at him, but I think they believe he is crazy or perhaps retarded. Someone tossed him an old tunic to wear and I can see him sitting in the village now. The children are trying to play with him, but he will not respond."

"Just go in and snatch him."

"I dare not. I would risk harming humans who I believe would try to defend him."

"Then go in and claim him as your slave," Wayne said urgently. "You speak German and he doesn't. They'll have to take your word for it."

"If they are not persuaded, then I shall have revealed my presence for nothing. That may be unwise."

"Well, then how do you want to handle it?"

"For now, I shall observe him further," said Ishihara. "I shall act when I am most comfortable under the Laws in doing so."

"All right. I can't argue with that," Wayne said reluctantly. "Give me some idea of which direction you went. I'm going to make camp for the night near the river. You get hold of MC 3 and we'll join up tomorrow."

"Agreed." Ishihara described his route after he had left Wayne.

"Good. Signing off." Wayne suppressed a smile as he switched off his communicator and returned to Steve. If he had had the help of a robot during his first two missions, he might have succeeded then.

"Have a nice visit with the underbrush?" Steve sneered.

Wayne was in a better mood now and ignored his tone. Leaving the rope tied to the tree, he moved cautiously to Steve's side. He saw that the loop still held Steve's upper arms tightly against his torso. "I'll help you down."

"Sounds good to me." Steve swung his leg over the horse and jumped to the ground, where Wayne steadied him. "All right, now what?"

"I'm going to see if I can get a fire started for the night, even though everything seems drenched."

"Good luck," Steve said doubtfully. "Look, at least untack the horse and hobble him. He shouldn't be tied up that way all night."

Wayne paused. He didn't know if Steve could get loose, but he was sure that it was possible somehow unless he was careful. However, unsaddling the horse would make Steve's escape on horseback less likely, so Wayne did not doubt his motive for making this suggestion.

"Yeah. That's true." Wayne looked at the bridle for a moment. It had an ordinary buckle on the side of the horse's head. Carefully, he unbuckled it and found that he could slide the bridle easily over the animal's ears and off its head. Then he studied the strap that ran under the horse's abdomen to hold the saddle in place.

"Ignore the wide part," said Steve. "That's the girth. Just loosen the cinch—that narrow leather strap up by the bottom edge of the saddle."

Wayne found the strap, which had been threaded in and out of a metal ring. When he pried the strap loose, the cinch and girth fell to the ground. Then he grabbed the saddle and pulled it off.

All afternoon, while riding with Wayne, Steve had flexed his arm muscles and unobtrusively strained against the loop that bound his upper arms. He could actually bend his elbows and move his hands, but that was not enough to loosen the loop now that the rope was soaked through with rain. Hoping to lure Wayne into letting down his guard, he had decided to be cooperative until a good opportunity to escape eventually developed.

Wayne was not a difficult captor. After hobbling the horse, he untied the free end of the rope holding Steve and let Steve have a moment of privacy in the bushes on the long leash; then he tied that end firmly around the base of a tree, where he sat to guard the knot. Steve sat against another tree, but he had a considerable radius in which he could move, either to sit and

The now-famous prototype of the highly successful "Hunter" class robot first demonstrated his remarkable abilities in the Mojave Center Governor case. The following images are drawn from the Robot City archives of Derec Avery, the eminent historian on robotics.

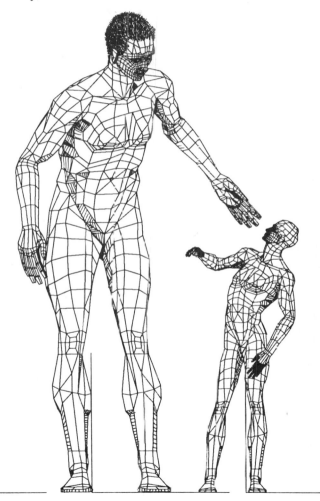

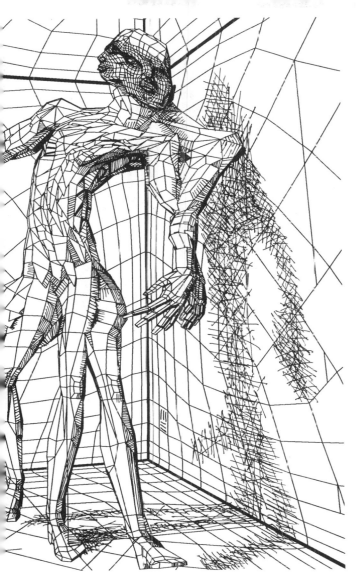

MC1 and MC2 merged. Two of MC Governor's six independent component robots are shown here. After capturing them in the remote past, R. Hunter merged and deactivated the robots temporarily.

The Bohung Institute. The famed Center for Robot Studies was founded in this underground university. Shown here is a view of the Institute's well-known towers, from which MC Governor launched his flight into the past.

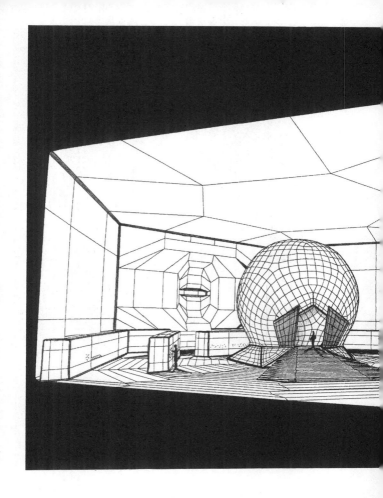

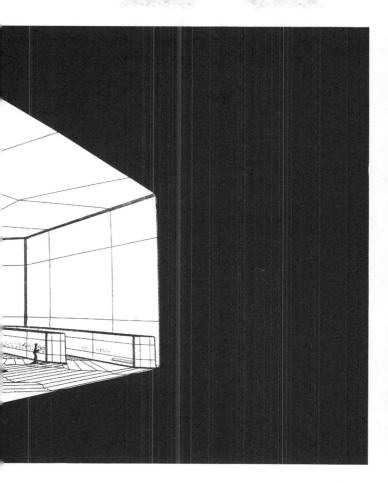

Room F-12 of the Bohung Institute. This view through a tower window shows the time machine used by R. Hunter and his team to search for Mojave Center Governor Robot.

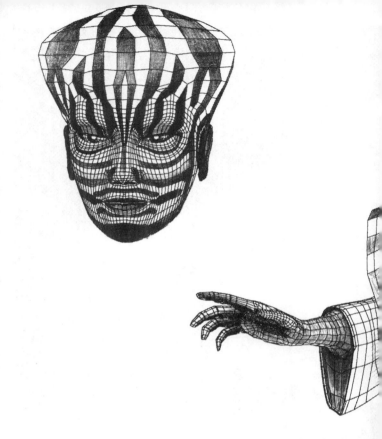

Three views of R. Ishihara. This robot's versatility made him a difficult opponent for R. Hunter. Originally in the service of the Bohung Institute, R. Ishihara was tricked into helping Dr. Wayne Nystrom in his attempts to foil R. Hunter's mission.

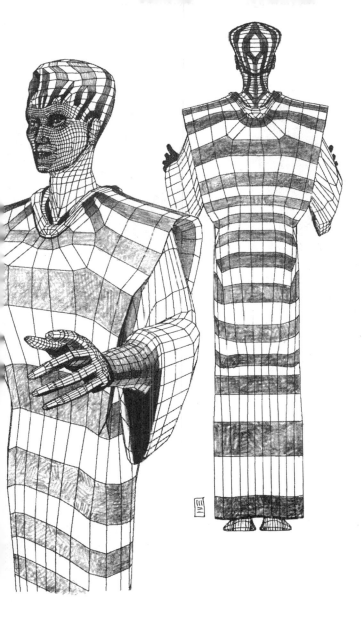

Exchanging Gifts in the German Camp. R. Hunter's versatility allows him to blend quickly into diverse cultures and situations. Here, he participates in a ritual exchange of valuables with a Germanic tribal leader.

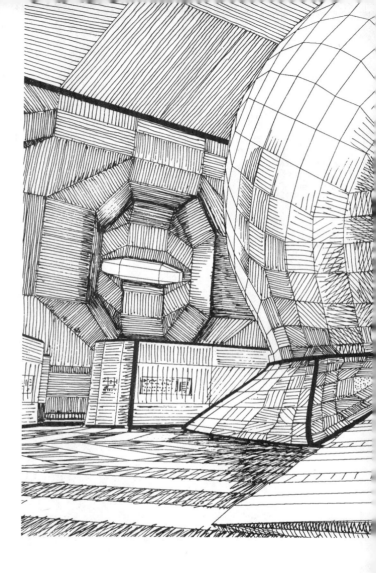

Returning With MC3. In this close-up of the time sphere in the Bohung Institute, R. Hunter and his team can be seen bringing the fugitive robot MC3 back to Mojave Center. The controls can be operated independently of the time sphere, so no operator is necessary when R. Hunter and his team leave and return from their missions.

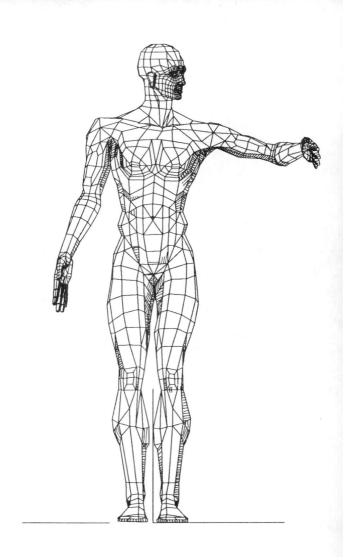

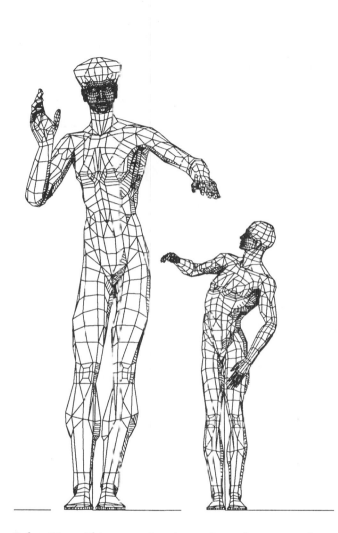

Robot Sizes. This composite picture shows the comparative sizes of R. Hunter, R. Ishihara, and MC3, one of the governor robot's six component robots.

Catching a Horse. R. Hunter carefully picked his supporting team of human experts. Here, Steve Chang, R. Hunter's wilderness survival expert, lassoes a fleeing mount.

lie down or even stand up to stretch his legs. He just couldn't reach the knot or free his upper arms. The rain lessened to a light drizzle, and under the heavy forest canopy, they were reasonably well sheltered.

Steve sat quietly, watching Wayne. He was especially surprised when Wayne opened the leather bag he was carrying on a thong. Wayne took out a lighter and poured a small amount of lighter fluid into it. Then he gathered up the least damp of the dead leaves and twigs around them, those which had been sheltered from the constant rain and drizzle under dense bushes or overhanging rocks.

Wayne carefully and slowly lighted a tiny, smoky fire and placed more wet kindling near it to dry off. Steve realized that in some way, Wayne had returned to the future. The rope and the leather bag could have been obtained either in Jamaica in the 1600s or here in this time, but that lighter had been manufactured many centuries in the future.

Steve spent the evening tied to the tree, fairly comfortable in the heavy furs that Vicinius and his father had provided. Wayne slowly and meticulously built up the fire and actually kept them both warm. He shared some packaged food of a familiar brand with Steve, but Steve decided not to comment on the fact that Wayne had obviously returned to their own time to get it.

Steve could not figure out how Wayne had managed to do that. Ishihara had been instructed to grab him if he reappeared in Room F-12. Clearly, however, Wayne had returned somehow and had remained free to come back to the forest.

Neither one of them talked. As the evening wore on, Steve grew sleepy; he had spent an active day out in the cold rain and the warmth of the fire made him drowsy. He lay down and closed his eyes, but he listened carefully for the sounds of Wayne's occasionally placing more sticks on the fire. It hissed and sputtered from rainwater dripping from the trees above, but Wayne was still working to keep it going.

After a while, Steve became aware that he had not heard Wayne feed the fire for some time. He opened his eyes. In the small circle of yellowish firelight, he saw that Wayne was lying down, using the leather bag as a pillow, breathing slowly. The fire had shrunk.

Steve wriggled slowly toward the fire, carefully stopping whenever he rustled dead leaves or twigs under him. Since the ground was damp, the noises were not very loud. Wayne remained asleep and Steve was able to roll up against the glowing embers on the edge of the dying fire. With the heavy fur cloak protecting his arms, he did not hesitate to move the rope holding him up against one of the red coals.

Soon Steve could see that the rope was slowly drying out. Then it began to darken and smolder. At the same time, the stench of singed fur also rose up from the spot.

He turned his face away from the unpleasant smell. Otherwise, he held his position and hoped the burning fur would not awaken Wayne. However, Wayne did not stir.

When the rope finally caught fire, it burned very fast. The loop fell away and Steve sat up promptly, away from the fire. Still careful to be quiet, he untied the free end of the rope from the tree.

Steve wanted to reverse the situation and tie up Wayne. Holding him for Hunter would make the rest of their missions much easier. He also had to get his communicator pin back so he could contact Hunter.

Walking carefully, he moved around the fire toward Wayne, tying a new loop in the end of the rope. Since that had worked to hold him, he knew he could hold

Wayne the same way. The problem was getting it over him.

"Hail, stranger," said a man's voice in German right behind him.

Startled, Steve whirled around. Several German warriors were just barely visible in the firelight. He recognized a couple of them. They were from Vicinius's village and were armed with spears.

"Hail," said Steve, uncertainly.

Suddenly Wayne rolled over and scrambled up, grabbing his leather bag. Steve spun toward him again and threw himself at Wayne's legs in a flying tackle, the looped rope hanging around one arm. He snagged one of Wayne's ankles and they both went down, but Wayne kicked free and slipped away.

Steve got up and started after him. Two steps into the brush, however, the rope caught on a tree branch, yanking his arm sharply. He came to a sudden stop.

As Steve turned and pulled his arm free, he could hear Wayne crashing through the underbrush. He doubted he could catch up with him, and he was concerned about the German warriors. With a self-conscious grin, he looked up and shrugged.

"Your name is Steve?" The leader of the group tapped his chest. "I have taken the name Flavius." He nodded toward the direction Wayne had taken. "We have interrupted something. He is your enemy?"

"Uh, yeah, he is."

"Shall we track him for you? He cannot have gone far."

Steve was tempted to accept the offer, but he was afraid these barbarians might be too rough on Wayne. All Steve wanted to do was get him into Hunter's custody and back to their own time. "No. He's not that important. But, uh, can you take me back to the village? I'm sort of lost."

Flavius turned and conferred quietly with his companions for a moment. Then he nodded to Steve. "Of course. We were on our way down the river tonight when we saw your campfire, but you are the guest of Vicinius and our chief, Odover. We will return to the village with you."

"Thank you. I'd like that." Steve grinned with relief. "But maybe you could help me find my horse. He's hobbled around here somewhere."

"Of course," said Flavius.

Night was just falling when Vicinius led Hunter and Gene back to the river. Before they actually left the trees for the river bank, however, Vicinius stopped.

"I hear horses," he said. "That means Romans are present. I do not wish to speak with them."

"No Roman will harm you while we are with them," said Hunter, firmly. "I am sure of that. Also, I have heard their voices nearby. Jane is riding one of the horses we hear. We must meet her."

"I understand." Vicinius gave an abrupt nod. "I am glad she is well. I will return to the village now. You can find it on your own?"

"Yes."

"Farewell. I will look for you later in the village." Vicinius slipped away into the woods.

Hunter could not worry about him. In fact, this was good, because he did not want to cause more Roman and German contact than they had historically experienced. He nodded to Gene and started down the trail.

Jane and a Roman officer rode into view out of the trees a moment later.

"Hail, Jane," said Hunter.

She laughed. "Hail, Hunter. Good to see you. This is Marcus, a Roman tribune. Marcus, this is the rest of my party, Hunter and Gene."

"Hail, Tribune."

"I give you greeting," said Marcus formally. "I am Marcus Gaius Aemilianus."

"Greetings," said Gene.

Jane was looking around anxiously. "Hunter, Steve isn't with you?"

"No," said Hunter.

"Something's wrong. We left him to meet you and started back for the fort. Then I . . . got worried." Jane pointedly tapped her communicator pin.

"I understand," said Hunter.

"I . . . turned around and came back, and Marcus was good enough to follow me." Jane shrugged helplessly.

"She is very strong-willed," said Marcus. "But I would not let her ride off alone. I must warn all of you, however, that the mood of the Cherusci is hostile. I suggest that we return to the safety of our camp."

"Thank you for your concern and dedication," said Hunter. "We are glad that Jane is safe."

"Her slave was mounted. He may well have found his way back to the camp on his own."

"Where did you leave him?" Gene asked.

"At the riverbank, right behind us just a few yards," said Jane.

"What about his tracks?" Hunter asked. "He must have left tracks in the mud there."

"It was too dark to see them when we got here," said Marcus. "And now we must return to camp."

Hunter knew that he could not argue very hard with Marcus without behaving unlike a trader from Gaul. On the other hand, he could not ignore Steve's disappearance. He was certain that Steve must have had a surprise confrontation with some German warriors, or possibly even some Romans. That meant that Hunter could not risk calling him on his communicator, for fear the others would overhear him.

"Thank you, Tribune," said Hunter. "Please take Jane and Gene back to your camp."

"You should come, too." Marcus spoke with the authority of an officer accustomed to obedience.

"I shall be fine," said Hunter patiently. "We appreciate your concern, Tribune. Please see that Jane and Gene are safe for the night. I fully expect to rejoin all of you with Steve in the morning."

"How can you search in this darkness?" Marcus demanded. "With these clouds we've had all week, no moonlight is going to help you. Searching at night is a waste of time."

"We deeply appreciate your hospitality," said Hunter. "I shall be fine."

"I must insist—"

"Let's go," Jane said to Marcus. "Arguing with him is a waste of time. He'll be all right."

"You two are much too fond of this slave," said Marcus, shaking his head. "Come on, then." He stretched an arm down toward Gene, to help him mount.

Gene took his arm and tried to jump up behind Marcus. Hunter stepped forward and helped lift him all the way up. When Gene was secure, Marcus turned his mount and rode away, with Jane behind him.

Hunter was worried about Steve, but at least he was free to stop his masquerade for the benefit of Vicinius or Marcus. He moved down the trail and magnified his vision to maximum light reception. Enough moonlight showed through the clouds for him to find his way, and he quickly found the tracks where Steve had walked his horse to the river and back. He also identified the spot where Steve had apparently fallen and been dragged into the woods.

From there, the horse's tracks led downstream. He followed them until they led him into forest. Under the trees, the forest was simply too dark even for Hunter's considerable light sensitivity. Marcus was right; he could not track Steve here in the darkness.

Hunter considered his options. He could still go to the Roman camp, arriving a little late, but it was clear from the tracks that Steve had not gone in that direction. The next morning he would be starting the search over again.

He could also spend the night where he was and begin the search from his present location at first light. As a robot with ample energy stored, he would be safe, especially under the forest canopy. He could even shut himself down except for his emergency communicator reception.

Hunter decided to take his final option, and return to the village of Vicinius and Odover. He had stored all of his movements around the forest in his memory, giving him a local map of any area he had seen. In such poor light, finding his way through the forest would be slow and clumsy, but in the village he could at least maintain his rapport with Vicinius. On the way, he would turn up his hearing for any sign of Steve.

He turned to orient himself and began the hike through the forest to the village.

Jane was very cold and tired by the time Marcus led them into the new Roman camp. It was laid out exactly like the previous one. The sound of falling axes she had heard was reflected in the new palisade wall surrounding the camp. The courtyard was lighted by torches placed around the inside of the palisade and she gratefully reined up behind Marcus and Gene at the stable. Her fur cloak had kept most of her dry, but her leggings and boots had been soaked through with rain by midday and her lower legs and feet ached with the cold. She dismounted with relief when the groom came to hold her bridle.

"To the governor's tent," Marcus said abruptly. He marched quickly toward it.

Gene grinned at Jane. "It's been a long day."

She smiled weakly, nodding.

At the entrance to the governor's tent, a sentry saluted Marcus and drew the flap open for him. Marcus stepped inside and saluted, while Jane and Gene stopped behind him, still out in the rain.

"Come in, Tribune," said Governor Varus. "Are your companions with you?"

"Yes, Governor." Marcus moved out of the way and gestured for them to follow him.

Jane slipped inside first and made room for Gene. The tent was lighted with four standing oil lamps, burning brightly in each corner. Governor Varus, warmly dressed in heavy woolen tunics, sat in a backless chair and sipped from a goblet of wine while Demetrius cleared the dishes from the table.

"This is the coldest, foulest night we've had yet this year," said Governor Varus, gesturing to the oil lamps. "Please warm yourselves. Demetrius, bring their meals."

Jane eased back her hood and shook out her hair, then held her hands near the flames. Gene joined her. Marcus moved to one of the other lamps to do the same.

"I'm glad you caught up with us again. It wasn't too difficult, I trust." Governor Varus looked up at Gene. "This must be your lost friend."

"No, sir," said Marcus. "This man is called Gene Titus. He is one of the lady's party from Gaul. Gene, this is Governor Varus of this province."

"Pleased to meet you," said Gene.

"Good evening. Come in and get warm. You are welcome here, of course."

"Thank you."

"But where is your slave?" The Governor addressed Jane. "Tending the horses or something of that sort? Yesterday, he hardly left your side."

"He didn't come back with us."

"No? What happened to him?"

"Her slave is now lost in the forest," said Marcus. "For her sake, I hope he is well."

"So, Tribune," said Governor Varus. "Bad fortune in finding your lost friend, eh? The one you started searching for in the first place."

"Worse than that, sir," said Marcus, unstrapping his helmet and pulling it off.

"Eh?"

"Late this afternoon we were confronted by a band of Cherusci warriors."

Governor Varus raised his eyebrows. "Go on."

"Governor, I am certain that trouble is on the way," said Marcus.

"Why are you so sure?"

"They had no particular business there by the river and frankly, they had nothing to say." Marcus set his helmet down at his feet and continued warming his hands. "Foul climate," he muttered.

"What *did* they say?"

"Virtually nothing," said Marcus. "But they made a point of coming out of the trees to be seen."

Governor Varus chuckled and sipped his wine. "That hardly constitutes a rebellion, Marcus."

"It was a small show of force to a lone tribune out with a civilian."

"Or perhaps it was a chance meeting in the forest and nothing more."

"Some kind of trouble is brewing, sir."

Demetrius entered with a tray of food and began laying it out on the table.

"Oh, I doubt it. After all, that's rather routine." Governor Varus held out his goblet for Demetrius to refill. "Sit down, please, all of you. Marcus, I shall listen to you as all of you warm up and enjoy your dinner."

"Marcus, you simply expect too much from these barbarians," said Governor Varus.

Jane and Gene took their seats. Marcus sat down last, sighing wearily. Demetrius moved behind Governor Varus and stood patiently.

"Let's ask our guests." Governor Varus turned to Jane. "You saw these Germans?"

"Yes, sir."

"Did they threaten you in any way?"

"No," Jane said hesitantly. She was aching to warn him, to convince him of the disaster he would fall into very soon. The reason was not that she had a great liking for the Romans as a group, but simply because she was uncomfortable knowing that so many Romans would soon be walking into a trap. Now that she was actually talking to two of them, they no longer seemed like mere historical figures. Of course, she knew she could not say anything that would even hint that Marcus was right. Instead, she would have to remain as neutral as possible, so as not to influence these two Romans.

"No. Were they armed?"

"They had spears," said Jane. "That's all I remember." She picked up her wine goblet, as much to hide behind it as to drink from it.

"That's often all these barbarians have," said Governor Varus calmly. He turned to Gene. "How about you? Did you see them?"

"No, Governor. I had not joined them yet."

"I see. Then let me ask the two of you another question entirely."

"Of course," said Gene.

"Perhaps I have been too hard on my tribune," said Governor Varus. "As I understand it, you have come here from Gaul, which means you passed through much of this province."

"Yes, sir," said Gene, watching him carefully.

Jane was glad to let him field the questions. After all, as the historian on the team, he had the best chance to pass as a real trader. She was too nervous to feel hungry, but she forced herself to eat, in order to keep busy.

"So in your travels, how were you received?" Governor Varus asked. "You must have visited many villages of the Cherusci before you got here."

"We were welcomed," said Gene. "At that time, we had a few modest gifts to present to the village elders."

"Ah, yes. They are sometimes like children with new playthings. Did they talk to you about us Romans?"

"Not particularly," said Gene. He looked at Jane innocently. "Do you recall?"

"No." She shook her head.

Governor Varus nodded.

"I'm afraid I'm quite ignorant of political matters," said Jane. She was sure that Romans of this time would accept that readily from a woman.

"German hostility has never died," said Marcus, looking up from his plate. "They like to buy our goods, but that's all. I suppose they see you traders as their friends, where we soldiers will always be their enemies."

"Where were you stationed before you came here?" Jane asked Marcus, hoping to turn the conversation away from the German rebellion.

"In Rome itself," said Marcus. He caught her eye and grinned at her. "The climate is so much nicer there. Have you ever been to Rome?"

"No." Jane suppressed a smile. She had been to Rome in her own time, but it was not the Rome Marcus knew.

"Have you seen the emperor?" Gene asked, sounding excited by the prospect.

"Oh, yes," said Marcus. "My cohort marched past him in review several times. I saw Emperor Augustus standing and watching us from a balcony."

"Marcus, I believe you may be making a conquest." Amused, Governor Varus stood up and slipped a heavy cloak over his shoulders. "Please continue your meal at your leisure. I wish to take a walk. Demetrius, remain here and see to them." He stepped out of the tent.

Jane watched Marcus, trying not to laugh at his embarrassment. To rescue him, she asked, "How about gladiators? Did you watch them fight?"

"Oh, yes," said Marcus. "It can be quite interesting. They are often very good, though of course it is not the same as soldiering."

"But they must be very good fighters."

"In their specialized duels, yes. For instance, one man will have a long net and a trident. He fights a man with a sword and a small shield." He frowned slightly. "The man with the net always seems to win. Those who assign the weapons dictate who lives and dies."

"You don't approve?" Gene asked cautiously.

"Soldiering is an honorable profession," said Marcus. "We serve the Empire. It requires discipline, teamwork, and duty. The gladiators are slaves."

Gene said nothing.

"You miss Rome, don't you?" Jane decided to change the subject.

"Yes, that is no secret. But a tribune can't earn the respect of his troops in Rome. For that, he has to go to the frontier and serve."

"The name Aemilianus is old and well-known," said Gene. "You must be well educated, I would guess."

"Yes. I learned Greek and studied the works of Homer and the great philosophers."

Jane remained quiet as Gene and Marcus discussed Greek philosophy. She probably knew a little more about it than most women of Gaul in this time, but the less she had to converse with Marcus, the better off she would be. When they had all finished eating, she waited for a moment when she could break into the conversation.

"I'm very tired," she said. "I'm afraid I'm not used to so much riding. I would like to go to sleep."

"Of course," said Marcus. "My tent is yours again. Uh, would you . . ." He glanced uncertainly at Gene.

"Our party normally remains together," said Jane.

"As you wish, of course."

As soon as Jane and Gene were in their tent, Jane called Hunter.

"Jane here. Can you hear me, Hunter?"

"Hunter here. Where are you, Jane?"

"Gene and I are in the new Roman camp. We don't know anything about Steve, though."

"I lost his tracks in the darkness," said Hunter. "I am slowly moving back toward Vicinius's village. I shall resume my search in the morning. You two are well?"

"Yes, we're fine."

"I am glad. Please call me in the morning when you can. Since you are in the Roman camp, I shall not risk calling you. Hunter out."

Ishihara spent the early evening outside the village into which MC 3 had gone. MC 3 continued to play with the children, tossing sticks and running through the village with them. He was clearly trying to establish a rapport with the villagers and the adults were simply ignoring him.

As Ishihara observed MC 3 from the forest, he also carefully watched the village dogs to see if they caught his scent. They did not. In part this was because, as a robot, he did not have a normal human scent and partly because the constant rain had driven the dogs into the huts.

He waited patiently as the villagers called their children and carried their dinners into the huts, out of the rain. Two of the children carried a bowl of food to MC 3, which he accepted, though he stayed a polite distance away from all the huts. He stood alone in the courtyard of the village, waiting patiently.

Eventually the families came out to douse their cookfires and begin chasing the children into the huts. One of the older children gestured for MC 3 to come in, too. MC 3 looked hesitantly at the father of the child, who nodded offhandedly for him to join them.

Ishihara noted which hut MC 3 entered. He was not entirely sure of what he would do, but this was his best chance yet to approach MC 3 without a crowd of humans who might protect him. Ishihara hoped to grab MC 3 somehow without risking a First Law violation by struggling with humans.

The village elders left sentries posted around the village when the rest of the villagers went inside for the night. For a while, the sentries paced about, talking and looking around under the sputtering torches they each carried.

As the night wore on, however, the sentries sat down around one small fire that remained lighted, feeding it occasionally. One of them pulled out an earthenware jug and passed it around. One by one, each sentry gradually leaned back against a tree trunk or stretched out under the overhanging thatched roof of a hut and dozed off.

Ishihara suspected that sentries were not normally posted in the village at night. He had overheard some of the conversation held by Hunter's team before they had left for this mission and he knew that trouble between the Germans and Romans was coming. That would explain the presence of the sentries. It also explained their carelessness.

When all the sentries had had time to fall into a fairly deep sleep, Ishihara slowly and patiently began moving toward the village. He was still concerned about the village dogs, too, but the constant spattering of the rain on the trees and the huts and the ground helped disguise the sound of his movements. In the darkness, with a care that few humans had the patience for, he took one step at a time toward the village.

Ishihara spent almost an hour moving thirty yards through the dense forest. Neither the sentries nor the dogs stirred.

Now that Ishihara was in the muddy clearing in the center of the village, he was more concerned about the excellent hearing of the dogs in the huts. He paused and magnified his hearing. The sentries and all the other humans he could hear were breathing deeply and evenly.

The villagers were not likely to be awakened by a slight sound. The breathing of the village dogs varied much more. Then another sound reached him, the faint crackling and cracking of wood. It was very faint and came from the back of the hut into which MC 3 had gone.

Certain that MC 3 was escaping, Ishihara abandoned his concern over making noise and ran around the hut. After the first hard, wet slap of his footsteps, the loud snap of wood breaking came from the back of the hut. Dogs began to bark all over the village and a couple of sentries called to each other in rough, surprised voices. Ishihara heard the sentries' wet, splashing feet as they ran after him.

Behind the hut, a flash of one of the torches carried by the lead sentry allowed Ishihara to glimpse MC 3 disappearing into the forest. A quick glance at the back of the hut told him that MC 3 had simply broken through a plank in the rear of the hut to

escape. Ishihara ran after MC 3, suddenly realizing
that MC 3 must have turned his own robotic hearing
up to maximum in order to detect the slight sounds
Ishihara had made as he approached the hut.

"I am R. Ishihara, a humaniform robot," Ishihara
radioed to MC 3. "I order you to stop under a First
Law emergency." He repeated the message, but he
could hear that MC 3 was still crashing through the
underbrush ahead.

MC 3 probably had kept his communicator shut off.
Ishihara also shouted the message a couple of times,
but MC 3 did not respond. He might have shut off his
hearing as well.

Up ahead, Ishihara heard leaves suddenly move just
overhead. The sound of more leaves shaking and some
twigs snapping told him that MC 3 had jumped up to
a tree branch and was climbing overhead to escape.
Using his hearing more than his sight in the dark
forest, Ishihara followed MC 3 up into the trees.

Climbing through the dripping trees was slow and
difficult, but Ishihara quickly heard the German warriors behind him drop back. They were not eager
to pursue a mysterious intruder in the dark. After
shouting angrily into the night, they returned to the
village.

MC 3 was moving from one tree to the next either by
jumping and grabbing another branch or by swinging
hand over hand between branches. Ishihara followed
him by doing the same. He was taller than MC 3
and had an advantage in both arm reach and overall
strength. Little by little, he gained on his quarry.

Ishihara heard MC 3 suddenly drop in three controlled jumps from branch to branch back to the

ground. Caught off guard, Ishihara moved back down more carefully, losing ground as he did so. Because he weighed considerably more than MC 3, fewer branches could bear his weight.

As soon as he was on the ground, MC 3 darted through the forest on foot. Ishihara finally jumped to the ground and ran after him. In the darkness, Ishihara could see virtually nothing. He was not specialized for a search, the way Hunter was, and lacked the infrared vision which would have allowed him to glimpse MC 3 by the heat he generated in the cold forest. He could, however, hear that MC 3 was also having trouble fleeing in the dark. Neither one of them was moving very quickly.

Ishihara heard branches snapping up ahead as MC 3 crashed into a bush, then a slapping sound as he fell onto the wet ground. Focusing on the noise, Ishihara took two more quick strides and blindly threw himself forward. With one hand, he snagged MC 3's ankle and held on.

MC 3 tripped, got up, and tried to scramble away. Ishihara's grip was firm, however, and he got to his feet, yanking MC 3's foot out from under him at the same time. MC 3 fell, with Ishihara still holding his ankle.

"Listen to me," Ishihara said aloud. He repeated the statement through his communication link, but MC 3 did not respond. Ishihara decided that trying to communicate was a waste of time and energy. He bent down to grip MC 3's right arm and released his ankle. Then he pulled MC 3 to his feet.

MC 3 was not resisting now, but he was tense, ready to run again if he thought it was worth the effort.

Ishihara did not have the device that triggered the time travel sphere. Wayne had kept it. Ishihara would have to join him with MC 3 before they could return to their own time.

Wayne had told him not to call him. Ishihara turned toward where he had last known Wayne to be and began to work his way in that direction. In his firm hold, MC 3 walked with him, not struggling.

Wayne had plunged through the forest in a panic to escape Steve when the German warriors distracted him. He had slammed his forehead into a low-hanging branch and fallen several times. Twice he had crashed into bushes and flailed blindly to get free. Finally, lost in the dark and out of breath, he had realized that no one had chased him.

When Wayne heard Steve lead his horse away with the Germans, he returned to his dying fire. He built it up slightly and lay awake in the wet forest for a long time, listening for more trouble. Finally, however, he stretched out and went to sleep again.

At dawn, he awoke stiff with cold but somewhat rested. The sky was gray but the rain had stopped for the moment. The fire had gone out and starting it again was too much work. He pulled a strip of commercially prepared beef jerky from his own time out of his pack and munched on it.

Wayne did not dare linger any longer. Steve could find Hunter and lead him back here. Wayne turned away from the river and began hiking in the general direction Ishihara had taken.

"I hate this," he muttered out loud to himself. "No matter what I do, something goes wrong." He reached for his communicator pin to call Ishihara.

After a hearty breakfast, Marcus rode out of the Roman camp with Jane by his side and Gene riding on the far side of her. He had agreed to help them search for Steve and their other lost friend. This time, he had taken one precaution. He had ordered a decury of cavalry, ten legionaries, to ride with them. Marcus did not intend to be caught unprepared again by any German warriors, and with everyone mounted, they would be able to run from a German force of any size.

He sneaked another glance at Jane, who had protested earnestly against his ordering the decury to accompany them.

"I confess you puzzle me," he said politely. "I should have thought you would be pleased to have a small squadron of cavalry to ride along this morning."

"You have been very courteous and considerate," said Jane. "But I really don't want to interfere with your army business."

"Oh, I think the Roman legions can manage their business today without us," Marcus said lightly, smiling at her. "They are still on the march today, and ten fewer cavalrymen will not even be missed."

Jane smiled tightly and glanced at Gene. "Maybe Gene and I should go out on our own. I would prefer not to trouble you any more than we have already."

"It would not be a problem," Gene said.

"Nonsense," said Marcus. "You are no bother at all. I am happy to accompany you. With good fortune, we may chance across more German warriors today and learn something of their intentions."

"I hope we don't meet any of them," Jane said quietly, exchanging another glance with Gene.

"We have nothing to fear from a small party," said Marcus. "And a large number of Germans will not be mounted, so we can ride away from them. I assure you both that I will see to your safety."

"Thank you," Jane said, with a weak smile. "You're very . . . conscientious."

Ishihara had made very little progress during the night. MC 3 alternately went limp, tried to wrestle away, or grabbed tree trunks with his free arm or even his legs as Ishihara tried to pull him through the dark forest. Ishihara did not have any way to communicate verbally with MC 3, as long as the component robot kept both his communication link and his hearing shut off, nor would he have had the authority of the Second Law over MC 3 in any case. All he could do was push, drag, and pull the smaller robot with him.

At dawn, Ishihara was able to see well enough to avoid colliding with as many bushes and trees as he had been in the darkness. He located his own trail, leading from where he had left Wayne to the German village, and backtracked. By midmorning, however, he had still made only a little progress.

Ishihara considered calling Wayne several times, but could not justify it to himself. The Second Law required that he obey Wayne's clear instruction not to call him, and Ishihara could not yet make a firm interpretation of a First Law problem that would require him to violate it. Dragging MC 3 through the forest was difficult and time-consuming, but it did not imply any particular danger to humans that Ishihara could see.

Steve had been very relieved to return to the German village late at night. Vicinius's hut was much drier and warmer than the damp ground next to Wayne's campfire had been. As he shared breakfast with Vicinius on yet another gray, chilly morning, Hunter walked out of the forest to join them. After they had all exchanged greetings, Hunter politely accepted a bowl of hot gruel.

"You have not found your friends," said Vicinius. "In fact, since you first came to visit us, you have lost two more of your party." He grinned. "I have not been much help to you; I can see that."

"You have been an excellent host," said Hunter. He turned to Steve. "I am glad to see you well. Do you have a suggestion for finding Jane and Gene today?"

"Well, I might." Steve understood that Hunter was speaking in a kind of code because Vicinius was with them. He chose his words carefully in return. "I lost a good luck charm last night." He patted the spot where he usually wore his communicator pin. "And I was tied up briefly by an old adversary of ours. He took my . . . charm."

"You have an enemy in this forest?" Vicinius turned in surprise. "Do not fear. Tell us where to find him. My friends and I will slay him for you."

"Not a blood enemy," Hunter said quickly. "He is, uh, a fellow trader. We do not want him killed." He looked at Steve. "You *do* mean Dr. Wayne Nystrom?"

"Yes."

"We would like to tie him up and take him with us, however," Hunter added.

"Why?" Vicinius looked back and forth between them. "If he is an enemy, you must kill him. If he is a friend, you would not talk about him this way."

"He might know stuff we want to know," said Steve quickly. "We might learn something from him."

"Ah! So you want to torture him for information." Vicinius nodded his understanding.

"No!" Hunter said sharply. "We . . . would like to take him back to Gaul with us to discuss business."

"No, no," said Vicinius, now shaking his head. "You Gauls are too soft."

"Maybe we are." Steve laughed and watched Hunter to see how he would react.

Vicinius caught his look, however. "I will be glad to help you, of course. This man is your concern, not mine."

"Maybe Flavius can tell you where he and his friends found me last night," said Steve.

"Your tracks will be easy to find," said Vicinius. "The rain has let up since yesterday."

"I have a Roman horse," Steve said to Hunter. "Vicinius and I can ride while you walk."

"Excellent," said Hunter. "When will you be ready?"

"Any time," said Steve.

"I will get my spear," said Vicinius.

By midday, Ishihara had not yet reached the spot where he had left Wayne. MC 3's resistance had slowed him to less than half of his normal speed. The day had otherwise been uneventful. Then he picked up the distant sounds of humans moving on foot through the forest behind him.

Instantly, he shifted his hearing to maximum. The humans seemed to be following his trail. He suspected they were from the village he was fleeing. If they had started trailing him at dawn, they might have needed all morning to draw this close to him.

This was the rationale Ishihara needed to call Wayne. If he lost MC 3, then their mission to save their own timestream would be endangered again. "Ishihara calling Wayne Nystrom. Do you read, sir?"

He was still dragging and half-carrying MC 3 through the brush as he radioed his message repeatedly. When he finally realized that Wayne was not going to answer, he became more concerned, but could do nothing except keep going. Since the humans behind him were slowly gaining ground, he encircled MC 3's waist with his arms and lifted the smaller robot off the ground.

MC 3 still kicked and struggled, but Ishihara began carrying him, hoping to leave his pursuers behind. However, MC 3 grabbed a tree branch with both hands and hung onto it. Ishihara wrenched him free, but could see that he was not going to be able to move much faster than he had been already. He turned to look behind him, peering through the trees for a sign of the Germans.

"Help!" MC 3 shouted suddenly in modern English. "Help! This way! Over here!"

Ishihara yanked him forward, trying to run. MC 3 could not have heard their pursuit with his hearing shut off, but he had surmised their presence by

Ishihara's actions. Ishihara pulled and shoved MC 3, but did not accomplish much. The smaller robot was as persistent and stubborn as he was, driven by the Third Law of Robotics to protect himself.

Shouts rose up from the men behind them. The German warriors could not have understood MC 3's exact words, but they understood his panicked tone. Ishihara heard them calling encouragement as they came crashing through the brush toward him. He recognized the loudest voice as belonging to the warrior who called himself Julius.

Ishihara ran through his limited options. He could continue to wrestle with MC 3 and be surrounded by Julius and his warriors. If he did that, he would have to attempt convincing the Germans that he had the right to carry off MC 3. He judged the likelihood of success to be extremely poor. His other option was to release MC 3, keep away from the Germans himself, and attempt to recapture him later. This second option would allow him freedom to carry out future plans with Wayne Nystrom to help.

Ishihara let go of MC 3, who instantly ran back toward the humans pursuing them.

At the same time, Ishihara turned and ran as fast as he could through the forest. Without the help of a human who could impose the authority of the Three Laws of Robotics on MC 3, capturing him again was probably a waste of time. Finding Wayne again was his top priority.

"Ishihara, come in," Wayne said quietly, as he hiked through the woods. "You there?"

"Yes, Wayne."

"Let's keep it short so we don't get our messages intercepted. Report on MC 3."

"I had him in custody for most of the night. When local German warriors approached us, I released him."

"*What*? Why?" Wayne was horrified.

"They were about to stop us. MC 3 has befriended them in some way. I could not fight them off without risking violation of the First Law. I judged that rejoining you would give us the opportunity to take him into custody again."

"Well . . . I see. Where are you?"

"I am on my way back to where we separated."

"I'm not far from there," said Wayne. "I'm working my way toward you. Do you have a reading on my position yet from the radio signal?"

"I have an approximate one. Without being able to triangulate, I need to monitor your signal continuously for maximum efficiency."

"I can't risk that. I still don't want Hunter to chance across our signal. I'll call you again after a while and let you judge by the strength of the radio signal how much closer we are to each other."

"Understood."

"Wayne out." He indulged in a brief smile, despite the cold and the dampness, and marched on through the forest.

On his first time trip, back to the Late Cretaceous, he had actually got control of Hunter under the Second Law for a short time. That had brought him pretty close to gaining control of MC 1, until Hunter's human team members had interfered. Then on his second trip, back to Jamaica in the 1600s, he had been able to enlist the help of local buccaneers who had actually grabbed MC 2 for a while. He just hadn't been able to take him back to their own time himself. Now he could see that he had been wise to bring Ishihara, though it had been Ishihara's idea. A robot was the best help of all.

If Wayne could just avoid having Hunter find out that Ishihara was here and helping him, he would have a real advantage. Steve could only tell him that Wayne was here; he didn't know about Ishihara. Unless they ran across Ishihara out in the forest by chance, the only way Hunter could learn about Ishihara's presence would be to intercept their radio messages.

"Hey—am I asleep, or what? I can listen in, too," Wayne said to himself aloud. He fumbled for the communicator pin he had taken from Steve. It was the same as his own, except that it would already be set for whatever frequency Hunter's team had been using. He turned it on and pinned it on his shoulder next to his own. All he heard at first was static, but that would change sooner or later, assuming Hunter's team was in range. "I should have thought of this right away."

Wayne hiked for quite a long time. Twice, he called Ishihara to check their positions. They were quickly approaching each other.

"Hunter, Jane here." Her voice came over Steve's communicator pin.

Wayne stopped where he was, one leg over a fallen log, to listen.

"Yes, Jane."

"Gene and I are with Marcus, but this morning he ordered an entire decury to ride with us. I'm afraid we're really changing some people's lives here."

"Where are you now?

"We're riding back down to the spot where we saw you last night. I told the guys I need another private moment in the bushes; as the only woman here, I don't have to worry about anyone joining me. They're all very protective."

"Steve and I met again this morning in the village of Vicinius and Odover," said Hunter. "But look out. Wayne is here and he tied up Steve for part of last night, till Steve got away."

"That explains what happened to him. What about MC 3?"

"All we really know is that Wayne did not have him either, as recently as last night. MC 3 is still in the area somewhere."

"What do you want to do, Hunter? I can't talk much longer or they'll worry about me."

"We should reunite the team," said Hunter. "We shall move in your direction and try to meet you sometime today."

Wayne smiled to himself. Hunter was temporarily too distracted even to go after MC 3. He and Ishihara had a good shot at getting him first.

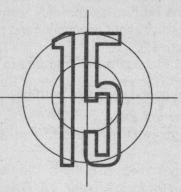

Jane rejoined Marcus, Gene, and the cavalry patrol with a cheerful smile and they all rode on. She had not had time to ask Hunter how he felt about the fact that Marcus had ordered the patrol to join them. Of course, she realized that the German rebellion was the major event that had to remain unchanged. This little patrol probably could not prevent that.

Marcus had ordered the decurion, the commanding officer of the patrol, to concentrate on the chore of finding their way. Meanwhile, Marcus had been talking with Jane. Normally, she would have been flattered by his attention, but she was so afraid of saying something she shouldn't that she did not want to speak.

"I have never been to Gaul," said Marcus. "Do you like it there?"

"Yes," said Jane.

"What's it like?"

"Well . . ." She tried to remember what she could about the climate, but she had only visited France for a short time. "The south of Gaul is very warm."

"Along the Mediterranean, yes, it would be. Much like the Italian coast, I expect." Marcus looked up at the gray sky. "The drizzle should start again any time, I suppose. I wish we had the climate of the southern coast here." He grinned at her. "A lady like yourself should not have to suffer through this constant cold and dampness."

Jane smiled politely but said nothing.

"I hear Gaul has few towns, as we Romans would know them, except for the ones we built."

Jane glanced uncomfortably at Gene.

"That's true," said Gene. "Gaul is not too unlike Germany, except for Roman influence."

Marcus nodded politely, but turned to Jane again. "What sort of family do you come from? Do you have many brothers and sisters?"

"I'm one of nine," Jane said truthfully. "Five brothers and three sisters."

"Ah! No deaths in childbirth? And you have all lived to adulthood?"

"That's right." She suppressed a smile of amusement.

"You come from strong, healthy stock." He grinned at her in obvious approval.

"Yes, I guess so." She was tempted to reciprocate by asking him about his own family, but she decided against it. Marcus clearly liked her, and she could not encourage his friendship without risking a change in his behavior toward his duties.

"So tell me," said Marcus. "Do you come from a town in Gaul? Or a small tribal village?"

"I'm from a town," said Jane.

"Was your father a trader, also?"

"Uh, no."

"Tribune," Gene interrupted. "We've been riding over half a day. I thought we probably would have seen some German warriors by now."

"Yes, where are they?" Jane glanced at Gene gratefully. He apparently understood her predicament and was still trying to distract Marcus for her.

"I am sure they have seen us," said Marcus. "Our horses make enough noise to give them plenty of warning, especially in these numbers."

"Why haven't they come out to speak to us?" Jane asked, to prevent him from turning the talk to her again.

"They don't want to reveal themselves because today we have too many armed men with us."

"Wait a minute," said Jane, trying to sound as naive as she could. "You mean they've been watching us in secret?"

"Indeed they have."

"How do you know?"

Marcus pointed to a flock of birds suddenly fluttering out of the trees into the sky up ahead. "I believe some German scouts are withdrawing ahead of us, simply watching to see what we will do. The birds give them away sometimes."

"Maybe we'll join up with Hunter and Steve soon," said Jane. "Then we can stop troubling you."

"We should probably go back to Gaul," said Gene. "And not get in your way."

"Don't worry about the Germans today," said Marcus, with a grim smile. "Whatever the Germans are planning, I believe it is very big, even if Governor Varus won't listen to me. If the scouts watching us wanted to cause trouble, they would have started already, I think. And we're ready for them now."

Jane and Gene exchanged an uncomfortable glance but said nothing more.

They all rode in silence for a while. The cold wind rose again, and the gray clouds above them darkened. Drizzle began to fall, blowing directly into their faces.

"Perhaps someday I can take you to the coast of Latium, down the Tiber River from Rome," Marcus said to Jane. "It is so much nicer than this on an autumn day. I would like to show it to you."

Just as Jane lifted the hood of her cloak and tugged it forward, she heard a chorus of yells from the forest. In the same instant, a Roman bugler behind her sounded an alarm. When she looked around, she saw German warriors leaping and running out of the trees toward them, hurling spears and shooting arrows. She recognized the man in the lead as Julius, who had confronted Marcus the previous day.

Jane yanked her reins to move away. At the same time, the Roman patrol moved up to surround her and Gene. Their shields deflected the volley of spears and arrows. Marcus shouted orders she could not understand in all the other yelling.

She fumbled for her lapel pin and switched it on, knowing that none of the Romans or Germans were paying any attention. Before she could speak, a small figure, dressed in rags, caught her attention in the trees behind the line of Germans. MC 3, who was identical to MC 1 and MC 2, was trying to wrestle a spear away from a much larger German warrior.

"What's wrong?" Gene yelled. "Doesn't it work? Do you want me to call Hunter instead?"

"Hunter!" She kept her eyes on MC 3. "It's Jane! Emergency! Hunter?"

"Yes, Jane." Hunter's voice was calm but authoritative. "I am on my way, following your signal. Please explain. And do not disconnect, as I shall need a continuing signal from you in order to find you as quickly as possible."

Jane's mount was still prancing in the center of the struggling Romans. Everyone around her was shouting. She yanked on the reins, fighting to keep control. "Our group is being attacked by a bunch of German warriors—"

"How do the numbers match up on each side?" Hunter interrupted.

"Uh, almost equal. There are more Germans, I think, but not a lot more, and they don't have horses or armor. But, Hunter—MC 3 is with the Germans!"

"I am coming," Hunter said firmly. "Keep your pin switched on. You do not need to continue speaking; I have enough noise coming through."

"Did you get him?" Gene shouted. He ducked as an arrow whistled near his head. "What did he say?"

"He's coming!" Jane leaned down low, not sure of what to do. Between the moving, clashing bodies around them, she could still glimpse MC 3 in the trees, still trying to interfere with a German warrior.

"What should we do?" Gene was also down low against his horse's neck.

"Just wait! And hang on!" Jane saw MC 3 again and straightened up in her saddle. "MC 3! Stop and move aside! That's an order!"

MC 3 did not respond. She knew he probably had not heard her voice in the shouting of all the fighting men and the clanging of swords against shields. In any case, he was now responding to the First Law in a feeble attempt to minimize the violence occurring in front of him. A Second Law instruction would not deter him at the moment.

Around her and Gene, the outnumbered Romans still fought to protect them.

Steve was riding double with Vicinius, following Hunter through the forest, when Hunter suddenly whirled around.

"I need your horse," said Hunter, striding back to them. "I must go." He tapped his shoulder in the same spot where Steve had worn his lapel communicator.

"Uh—of course," said Steve, understanding that Hunter had received a call from Jane or Gene. "But, maybe we should all go together?"

"No, Steve. I must hurry. You will remain with Vicinius." Hunter reached up to take Steve under his arms; the big robot lifted him to the ground as if he were a small child.

Taking the hint, Vicinius jumped to the ground on his own.

"Vicinius," said Hunter. "I do not have time to explain. But you will protect Steve for me?"

"Of course," said Vicinius, clearly puzzled. "Of course."

"You may follow at your own pace, provided you are very careful. I shall rejoin you as soon as I can." Hunter mounted quickly and rode away through the forest, leaning low to avoid tree branches.

"I heard nothing," said Vicinius, with a mystified expression on his face. "I saw nothing. What is he doing?"

"I, uh, didn't hear anything, either," said Steve. "And I didn't see anything."

Vicinius turned to look him in the eye. "Then I ask you, what is he doing? What is so important that he must leave us this way?"

"Well . . . sometimes Hunter reads omens that the rest of us do not notice."

"Omens?"

"Yeah, I think so." Steve shrugged. "Not real often. But sometimes he just has to, uh, act on them."

"Your friend is more than a little strange," said Vicinius. "I like him, but he is quite strange."

"Come on," said Steve, hoping to change the subject. "We can follow him. Let's go."

As Hunter rode through the heavy forest, he radioed MC 3 again. He received no response, which did not surprise him. Jane no longer spoke to him directly, but her communicator was still transmitting. He heard the shouts of many men, the whinnying of horses, and the clanging of metal.

Before he got close enough to hear the sounds of struggle with his own hearing, rather than the communication link, the sounds of struggle coming over the radio stopped as well. For several moments, he heard only the clopping of horse's hooves.

"They're gone," Jane muttered quietly. "Gene and I are okay. Right, Gene?"

"Yeah," said Gene, his voice sounding distant in the background.

"Decurion," Marcus ordered, his voice even fainter. "Give me an injury report."

Hunter could hear the decurion respond, but the signal was now too faint even for him to interpret. He was deeply concerned about harm to any humans who would not have been injured without the presence of his team. For now, however, all he could do was hurry in their direction as fast as he could.

Before Hunter drew near the site of the attack, the source of the signal began to move, as Jane rode away with the patrol. Now that the sounds of battle no longer covered his voice, he did not dare speak to Jane again, nor could she say anything to him directly. However, she did continue a stream of small talk with Gene, which provided him with a clear, strong signal to follow. The Roman patrol had clearly changed direction; Hunter guessed that they were returning to the main body of Roman legions to avoid further trouble with hostile Germans.

Steve and Vicinius hurried after Hunter, but of course they had no chance of catching up until he stopped somewhere. When Hunter's tracks began to curve in a new direction, Steve guessed that Jane and Gene had begun to move, but he had no idea where they were going. As his determined strides gradually faltered from weariness, Steve decided to take a break.

"Sorry, Vicinius." He stopped near a fallen log. "I'm not used to this kind of mountain country. I have to rest for a few minutes." He sat down.

"Well . . . of course." Vicinius reluctantly joined him on the log. "Not too long, eh? Hunter is still gaining ground on us even while we're walking."

"All right. Not too long." Steve was sure that either Jane and Gene were in trouble or else MC 3 had been found; nothing else would have taken Hunter away like that. In either case, the imminent German rebellion might have influenced events. "Vicinius, do you know of any danger that might be out in the forest today?"

"The forest always has dangers—an angry wild boar, a mother bear protecting her cubs in the spring . . . in winter, a hungry wolf." He shrugged. "Even a challenge from another warrior, maybe over a woman."

"Uh—yeah. Well, I meant . . ." He trailed off, not sure what to say.

"You are wondering what omens Hunter saw?"

"I wish I knew, yeah." Steve grinned. "But that's not what I meant. We know the Roman legions are marching near here. I was wondering if trouble is on the way with them."

"The Romans brought trouble with them a generation ago," said Vicinius casually, looking away from Steve at nothing in particular.

"I guess you know they came to Gaul long before that."

"So I have heard."

"But the Gauls are used to the Romans now. Many even like the peace and prosperity they have brought."

"The Gauls are . . . not strong enough. With respect to your masters, of course. Hunter is a fine man."

Steve suppressed a grin. "He's quite a . . . specimen, all right. But I have the feeling that the Cherusci tribe are not as tame as the Gauls, where Romans are concerned. What do you say?"

"Yes! Yes, we Cherusci are becoming impatient. I will grant you that." Vicinius turned to look directly at Steve. "You are not a Gaul, but your masters are. They are my friends, but perhaps they are too fond of Romans for my own taste."

"Trouble is starting, isn't it?" Steve knew it was, of course, but in order to discuss the subject with Vicinius, he had to induce Vicinius to acknowledge the fact.

"Prince Arminius has been visiting each village for the past week or two," said Vicinius. "He has been our leader in dealing with the Romans."

"And?"

"He is rousing all the Cherusci villages. The men of my village will be moving soon. I will join them." His voice lowered. "I am telling you this as a friend. Maybe you can keep your masters away from trouble when it starts."

"I appreciate your trusting me."

Vicinius stood up. "I believe I can judge whether to trust a man or not. Let's go."

"Good idea." Steve got up and followed him through the forest.

When Wayne finally saw Ishihara walk around a large tree to meet him, he felt that he had found his only friend in the world. In this time period, in fact, that was true. He grinned with relief, but stifled an impulse to slap the robot on the back.

"I'm glad to see you," said Wayne.

"You are well?"

"Yeah, I'm okay."

"Good. What are your instructions now?"

"Well, you know who got MC 3 from you. Where is he now?" Wayne sat down against the base of a tree. "I'm worn out from walking all day."

"He is with a party of native Cherusci warriors led by a young man named Julius. They come from the village of Prince Arminius, the leader of the Cherusci."

Wayne tensed. "Yeah, I know that village. They didn't like me much."

"What do you suggest?"

"Hunter's team is still trying to reunite. I want to find MC 3 and take him home while Hunter is distracted."

"I agree. However, the only way to find him is to return to the outskirts of their village and wait for them to go home for the night."

"Why? Can't we find them out in the forest somewhere, instead?"

"It is too late in the day now to locate them," said Ishihara. "Besides, I have no idea of where they would be, except by tracking them. But we can rely on their need to return home by sundown."

"I know roughly where they were not too long ago," Wayne said quickly. "Maybe we can intercept them. I don't want to go anywhere near that village again."

Wayne tapped Steve's lapel pin. "I can monitor the radio communication between members of Hunter's team. A bunch of Germans attacked a Roman patrol while MC 3 was with them. They were over that way." He pointed. "From the strength of the signal, I don't think they were too far."

"Excellent," said Ishihara. "After a bout of combat, they will probably have returned early to tend their wounded or dead. They may be there already. I suggest we move in the direction of the village of Julius and Prince Arminius, despite your concern. I shall remain with you, or very close, to protect you under the First Law."

"Well . . . I guess if that's where MC 3 is, I don't have much choice. But I don't want to be captured by those German warriors again."

"I understand," said Ishihara. "I shall arrange a small fire and a lean-to for your comfort tonight, at a safe distance from the village. When you are comfortable, I shall attempt to observe MC 3 in the village this evening. I shall look for another opportunity to take custody of him, but I shall consult with you before taking any action."

"I still have some dried packaged food, but I'll need water."

"In this constant drizzle, I can provide enough water with no problem."

"Okay." Wayne got up wearily. "I can hardly wait to walk some more. You know the way?"

"I do."

Wayne gestured for him to lead.

The German warriors had fled from Marcus's patrol as suddenly as they had attacked. He understood; they were merely letting their presence be known, to intimidate him a little. The lightly armed Germans had done no significant harm to the well-armored, mounted Romans.

However, more certain than ever that a real rebellion was on the way, Marcus had led his patrol away from the site at a canter until the dense forest forced him to slow down. Before long, however, he located the section of muddy road that thousands of Roman legionaries had churned to slop on their march. Moving as quickly as the horses could handle the mud, he caught up to the Roman army again. They were just breaking formation, ready to begin making camp for the night.

The Roman army was still strung out along the road. The baggage wagons brought up the rear and drivers struggled to turn the teams of horses and move them off the road. In front of the baggage train, the infantry units marched away from the road to begin building the camp. The cavalry units had already moved into the trees.

The three of them rode slowly through the crowd of legionaries and baggage wagons to the front. There, Marcus found the tent of Governor Varus being raised in what would become the center of the camp. They were surrounded by legionaries shouting, giving orders, and hustling in different directions. Marcus leaped off his horse, looking around for the governor.

"Good day, Tribune," Governor Varus called, moving away from a crowd of officers. "You look rather excited, Marcus. Have any luck today?"

"I had a decury of cavalry with me," Marcus said quickly. "Governor, we were attacked by a small party of Cherusci. I wanted to report right away."

"Yes?"

"Well . . . we were attacked, not too far from the river. Not far from here, really."

"How far from here?"

"An hour's ride."

"By a small party?"

"Yes, sir."

"How many did we lose?"

"None, sir."

"None? How many of them did you get?"

"I believe we wounded most of them, but they got away."

"You lost none and killed none?"

"I believe that is correct, sir."

"Marcus, was this a fight or a folk dance?" Governor Varus smirked.

"Sir!" Marcus stiffened. "This was an attack by poorly armed Germans on a trained cavalry patrol, but it was a serious skirmish."

"Oh, Marcus, come on. How serious could it have been—a battle without one single unfortunate left dead on the ground from either side?"

"Their intent was to test our strength and our resolve," said Marcus. "They were serious about that."

"These minor tussles, Marcus, are merely the burden of the conqueror. They can be handled." Varus looked up at the sky. "This is the first excuse for a dry day we have had in some time, if you ignore a little drizzle. I want to take a quick walk among the troops to boost their morale, before that infernal rain starts again."

"But, sir, I really believe this skirmish is important." Marcus walked alongside the governor as he began to walk. "It means more than it seems."

"Marcus, I suggest you use this as a learning experience. For instance, what do you believe should be done?"

"I think we should send out a series of patrols right now and also at dawn, to find out if larger bodies of Germans have gathered elsewhere in these mountains."

Governor Varus laughed lightly, shaking his head. "Well, you are dedicated, Marcus; no one has ever doubted that. But I don't want to wear out a bunch of cavalry patrols on a wild-goose chase, not after those poor animals slogged through knee-deep mud in the road all day."

"But, sir—"

"I'll tell you what, Marcus," said the governor. "if you wish, take out a larger patrol and burn a German village in retaliation for their attack on your patrol."

"That won't bring the kind of large-scale information I was talking about, sir."

"That's *not* an order, Tribune. It is merely an option you may wish to exercise. Make your own decision."

"But, Governor—"

"Excuse me, Tribune. I believe I will mingle with the troops alone. See to your guests, eh?"

"Yes, sir." Marcus stopped, his fists clenched in frustration as Governor Varus walked away.

Jane remained mounted, at first, when Marcus cantered up to Governor Varus. When the grooms came forward to take their horses, she dismounted and stood with Gene, a polite distance away. When Governor Varus and Marcus began walking away, she and Gene remained where they were.

"How much could you overhear?" Gene asked.

"Only a little. But it sounds like Varus is so closed-minded that we don't have much to worry about."

"Keep your voice down about that stuff," said Gene, glancing nervously at some legionaries marching past them. "We can't afford to sound like security risks."

"Sorry. Look, Marcus is coming back."

Marcus's face was taut as he strode toward them. He was as courteous as usual, however. "The governor's tent is up. Let's go sit down."

Jane and Gene followed him into the tent, where Demetrius had already set up the furniture. He was just lighting the oil lamps to provide some light and heat. Marcus gestured for Jane and Gene to sit and collapsed into a chair himself.

"Wine, Demetrius," said Marcus roughly.

"Yes, sir. Would you like that heated, sir?"

"Yes, yes, of course." Marcus sighed, then slammed his fist down on the table angrily.

Jane sat down, loosening her cloak around her, and glanced at Gene, who was warming his hands over the fire.

"He has no idea," Marcus muttered. "Look, I have every respect for Governor Varus. But I just *know* he is missing something about these German tribes."

Jane nodded, afraid to say anything.

Marcus turned to Gene. "In many ways, he is a fine man, but he is taking Roman power for granted."

"We are merely traders," said Gene.

Demetrius entered with a tray of bread and mulled wine. He served it to the three of them in silence. Outside the tent, the men working to make camp shouted and called to each other. Marcus waved a hand for Demetrius to leave.

Jane tasted the wine carefully. After a day out in the cold, the warmth was welcome. The bread was not fresh, but it was better than nothing.

"I could burn a village," said Marcus. "I have the authority to do that."

"Burn a village?" Jane looked up.

"This is a normal form of retaliation." Marcus shook his head. "But in this case, it will simply spur greater resistance to us, and tell us nothing."

Gene joined the other two at the table, saying nothing as he tore apart a piece of bread.

Jane was more uncomfortable than ever.

Marcus looked at Gene. "Maybe you have had a leader who made a mistake at one time or another. How would you tell Hunter, for instance, that he is wrong?"

"Well . . . Hunter is quite reasonable. He is open to discussion."

Marcus turned to Jane. "You feel that way, as well? How would you speak to him?"

"Hunter can be persuaded, with enough evidence," said Jane, over her goblet of wine.

Marcus merely nodded and took another piece of bread. "You are fortunate."

They ate and drank in silence for a while. When the bread and wine were gone, Marcus brushed away crumbs and stood up. Jane rose too, waiting to see what he would say.

"Would you excuse me? You may remain here, of course, and be comfortable." Marcus waved to Demetrius, who was standing outside the tent. "Bring them more if they wish."

"I'm finished," said Jane.

"Thank you, I've had plenty, too." Gene got up and joined Jane.

"Very well," said Marcus. "As you wish, of course. Make yourselves comfortable." He ducked out of the tent and hurried away.

"Let's take a little walk," said Jane. She wanted to talk to Gene without Demetrius listening.

"Sure."

Outside the tent, Roman legionaries surrounded them everywhere, but everyone was occupied. Gene and Jane walked casually, staying out of the way of the troops and the work crews. In turn, they were ignored.

"Do you think we've really messed up?" Jane asked, pulling her cloak around her. "Have we caused Marcus to change his behavior significantly?"

"We have no way of knowing," said Gene, pausing to watch another tent being raised. "I never came across Marcus's name in my history, at least that I can remember. His actions may never have been written down by any historian."

"I'm just afraid that the Germans only attacked our patrol because Marcus took us out today. Anything that the Romans or Germans do as a result of that skirmish could mean a significant change."

Gene nodded. "I know, but look at it the other way. Maybe, even without us, Marcus or some other patrol might have gone out today and been in a skirmish with the Germans. Maybe it would have happened without us."

"Since MC 3 was with that bunch of Germans, I suppose they were somehow influenced by his presence, too."

"Sure, it's possible. But we can't know for sure. And now we can't undo it, either."

"And what if he goes out to burn a village in retaliation after all?"

"It doesn't sound like he really wants to. But he might have done that without us, too. After all, it's a standard tactic in Roman intimidation."

"Jane, Gene!" Hunter's voice reached them from behind.

Jane turned in surprise. "I'm glad to see you!"

"You are both well, I see."

"We're all right," said Gene. "But we're both worried about the changes we may have caused."

"It's Marcus," said Jane anxiously. "He's trying harder than ever to convince Governor Varus that the Germans are up to something."

"Because of the attack you told me about?" Hunter glanced around the camp.

"Yes."

"I understand. What more do you know about MC 3? You said he was with the German party?"

"Yes, but he kept trying to interfere with their fighting—to stop them under the First Law. They may not be very happy with him now."

"Yes, I agree," said Hunter. "He would have a hard time explaining his actions to them—even if he could speak their language, which I doubt. He remained with them after the combat had ended?"

Jane looked at Gene, shrugging.

"I couldn't see, either," said Gene. "But I suppose he is still with them."

As the legionaries and work crews continued to raise the camp around them, Hunter quickly reviewed his historical data. It did not contain enough detail to help him. "Gene, has the governor so far altered anything because of Marcus?"

"I don't think so," said Gene. "Marcus is very angry right now over his failure to convince Governor Varus that the Germans could be a real danger. That must mean the governor has not changed his orders."

"Good," said Hunter. "If the change has been confined to Marcus, then it may not matter. What about the Germans? Are they acting differently?"

"Sorry." Gene shook his head. "I'm afraid I can't help you there."

"No?"

"The historical records discuss the Roman failure to prepare for the ambush in Teutoburger Forest, and the attack itself," said Gene. "They really don't give much detail about German preparations. I suppose the

Roman historians never really knew too much about those details."

"I have no idea what influence MC 3 could have had so far," said Jane. "If he can't speak German, which is probable, he might not have had much at all. But if he displayed any robotic abilities that the Germans considered more than human . . ." She shrugged. "Anything could have happened."

"That's true," said Gene. "The Germans might have associated him in some way with their folk religion if he showed them any special abilities."

"I understand," said Hunter. "In the cases of both the Romans and the Germans, nothing critically important appears to have happened yet. The danger is that a small event or two will snowball."

"What do you think we should do?" Jane asked.

"I shall start by talking to Marcus," said Hunter. "Where is he?"

Jane looked around. "He was here just a minute ago—there." She pointed. "He's talking to some people."

"Thank you." Hunter saw Marcus talking to two other Roman officers. He approached them slowly, not wanting to appear to interfere.

"I'm only asking you to think about it," Marcus was saying to the other officers.

"It's this weather I'm worried about," one of them responded. "All we need is a mudslide or something on these horrible barbaric roads."

"After all," said the other. "You're the governor's aide, Marcus. If you can't convince him, I don't see how the rest of us can."

"Maybe if we all spoke to him, in a formal meeting—" Marcus started.

"Sorry," said one of the other officers. "I have no wish to risk my career on predicting the behavior of these savages."

"I would watch my tongue if I were you," said the other. "You don't want to make the governor doubt your judgment in the future."

The other two officers walked away. Marcus sighed and looked around. Hunter hurried up to him.

"Good evening, Tribune."

"Ah, Hunter. I wish it was. I'm glad to see you are well, however."

"I could not help but overhear part of your conversation," said Hunter. "I know that Roman army matters are none of my business, as a traveling trader, but would you like to talk, just between friends?"

"I could use a friend right now," Marcus said grimly. Then he grinned wryly. "No, that's too strong. Governor Varus has been a good mentor. But he just can't see what's right in front of him."

"Jane and Gene told me you had a clash with the Germans today. You feel more is to come?"

"I'm certain of it."

"Have they skirmished like this with you before?" Hunter asked. "You Romans, I mean."

"No, not recently. Not since Prince Arminius and the Cherusci tribe were given status with the Empire. That was before I received my assignment here."

Hunter nodded, trying to convey concern. "Would you have ridden out today, if Jane and Gene had not enlisted your help in their own search?"

"No, I don't think so. But I was glad to do it. Don't make any mistake about that."

"You have been very kind." Hunter considered what

little information he had. Knowing that he could make no more than a poorly educated guess, he estimated that so far, Marcus and the Germans had engaged in no more than a minor historical change. He simply had to stop the damage right away.

"It's nothing, Hunter. Besides, if I hadn't taken them out today, I would never have received further evidence of German hostility."

"What casualties were sustained? On either side?"

"None for us, except for a few scratches and bruises. I think we made a better showing against them, but they carried their wounded away."

"So perhaps no retaliation is really called for. You already got the best of them."

"Well . . . I guess you could look at it that way." Marcus grinned, finally.

"Tribune, I shall tell my party that we shall not interfere with you any further. Your army duties must come first. I feel that we are entirely to blame for disrupting your normal routine. Please accept my apologies."

"Not at all, Hunter. I was glad to help. But I will respect your wishes, of course."

"I do not want to disturb you further," said Hunter. "I shall rejoin Jane and Gene."

"As you wish. You will all be my guests for dinner, of course." Marcus nodded and walked away.

Hunter returned to Jane and Gene, who were standing near the governor's tent.

"What do you think?" Jane asked. "Have we really made a bad mistake?"

"I told him we shall not interfere with army routine again," said Hunter. "If the German ambush of this army takes place as it should, then we have not caused irreparable harm to the sequence of events."

"What do you want us to do now?" Gene asked.

"I want to reunite the team," said Hunter quietly, looking around to make sure none of the Romans was close enough to listen. "However, attempting to bring Steve here tonight does not seem wise."

"Do you want us to go with you?" Jane tugged her cloak tighter around her. "We've had a long day, but if we have to go, then we have to go."

"No. I don't want to take you two away from the safety of the Roman camp for tonight."

"Are you going to go after him yourself?" Gene asked. "That means we split up again."

"Unwise, also, I think," said Hunter. "I cannot reunite the team by shuttling back and forth between you two and Steve. I shall spend the night here."

"Are you going to explain to him what's going on?" Jane looked out across the darkening forest. "Maybe we could make plans to meet tomorrow."

"No. Since Steve no longer has a communicator pin, calling him is not possible."

"Then our plan of action begins tomorrow," said Gene.

"Yes," said Hunter. "For now, we shall merely accept Roman hospitality and safety for the night."

Steve returned with Vicinius to his village with growing pessimism. They had basically wasted the day walking in a big circle. Steve was getting tired of wasting so much time looking for MC 3.

At least he found dinner hot and plentiful. That night he accepted a bowl of stew made from chunks of boar meat with a variety of nuts and grains. Steve supposed the latter had been part of the fall harvest. He sat with Vicinius and Odover at the fire in the waning sunlight, eating quietly.

The sound of a horse's hooves caused everyone to turn. A tall, burly German in furs rode bareback into the village, followed by a large party of German warriors on foot. He had shoulder-length blond hair and a proudly grim expression. Many of the villagers leaped up to greet him. Odover, the village chief, laid down his bowl near the fire and got to his feet slowly, with the dignity of age.

"Prince Arminius," Vicinius whispered to Steve quickly. "Remain here. Lately, he has not been fond of strangers who come from west of the Rhine."

Steve nodded. Vicinius jumped up and joined his father, walking to meet their new visitors. All through the village, people were running up to shout greetings to Prince Arminius, especially the young warriors.

Amid all the shouts, Steve had difficulty hearing what anyone was saying. Of course, he already knew the purpose of Prince Arminius's visit; he had to be gathering warriors for his attack on the Romans. Steve was surprised, however, to see that he was not just a loudmouthed rabble-rouser. Within several minutes, the villagers were standing quietly as he moved among them, greeting individuals and talking to them one at a time. Steve could see the warriors of the village pushing forward to hear him speak.

From the phrases and snatches of conversation Steve could hear, Prince Arminius was simply encouraging everyone, talking about the pride and strength of the Cherusci tribe. Other members of his entourage were doing the same, greeting friends of their own in the village. The warriors of Odover's village were excited and hoisted their spears in greeting.

Vicinius returned to Steve, grinning, and sat down with him again. "Prince Arminius is very popular. He is a brave warrior and leader. As the son of Odover, I had to greet him with my father."

"Of course. Don't worry about me. If you need to talk to the rest of them, go ahead."

"No, I am ready." He looked at Steve carefully. "We must drive the Roman soldiers from our country. A trading party, now, that is different. You come in friendship. But I am ready to answer Prince Arminius's call. And now I expect it to come soon."

Steve nodded. "I understand. No one wants to be ruled by others."

"Vicinius!"

Vicinius turned and looked up. "Hello, Julius."

"Hah. When we have run these Roman dogs out of our land, we will drop these Latin names again, eh?" Julius glared at Steve. "Who is this foreigner?"

"My guest," Vicinius said firmly. "He is seeking a lost companion, in fact. A short, slender man, touched by the gods and wandering in the forest. If you—"

Julius's eyes narrowed. "What about him?"

"You know where he is?" Steve stood up suddenly. "I need to find him."

"Vicinius, who is this man?" Julius demanded.

"He is Steve, the slave of a trader from Gaul." Vicinius got up, also, and pushed in front of Julius.

"A Roman spy, more likely." Julius shoved Vicinius aside. "And he has heard too much here tonight."

"I'm no spy," Steve said mildly, figuring that a slave

might be rather meek in the face of an angry warrior. "I've been separated from my—"

"I say you are!" Julius put a large hand against Steve's chest and shoved.

"Hey!" Steve slapped his hand away, stumbling backward from his assailant's greater weight.

"He is my guest!" Vicinius grabbed Julius's arm.

As Steve regained his balance, he saw Julius swivel and punch Vicinius in the stomach, catching him by surprise. While Vicinius fell to his knees, doubled forward, Julius reached for a large knife in the side of his leather belt. A few of the other villagers gasped in shock, but most had not yet even noticed the sudden action.

Steve knew instantly that he could not fight Julius hand to hand once the German warrior was ready. This was his only moment to strike. Just as Julius yanked the knife out, Steve launched himself forward in a flying tackle, grabbing Julius around the waist. Steve drove him backward and down.

The moment they landed on the cold, soggy ground, Steve rolled off and kicked Julius's hand. The knife rolled free, but did not go very far. Steve scrambled for it, but Vicinius snatched it up and stood, holding it in a fighting position as he faced toward Julius.

"Stop!" Vicinius ordered.

By now, other villagers had gathered around them. Their shouts of alarm and surprise had stopped as they watched to see what would happen next. Steve stood up and edged around behind Vicinius, eyeing Julius suspiciously.

"You will respect my guest in this village," Vicinius said coldly. He tossed the knife down at Julius's feet.

"Julius." Prince Arminius spoke firmly, striding through the crowd as others made way for him. "Save your energy for the Romans. We must go."

Steve said nothing as Prince Arminius turned with a swirl of his fur cloak and strode back toward his horse. Julius angrily grabbed his knife and stomped after him. Most of the crowd of villagers followed them.

"You are quick," said Vicinius. "I almost tossed you my own knife and just let you fight it out."

"Really?" Steve grinned wryly. "I'm glad you didn't. I'm no fighter."

"I had to stop him. Julius may not assault any guest of mine. You are under the protection of my hospitality here." Vicinius gave him a slap on the shoulder that jarred him.

"I think he knows something about MC 3," said Steve. "Did you see how he reacted? Can we find out?" He started after Prince Arminius and Julius.

"No. Not now." Vicinius grasped his arm and held it firmly, stopping him.

"Can you help? Maybe Prince Arminius—"

"No," he repeated with finality. "Prince Arminius is in no mood to talk about anything but war against the Romans. Nor will Julius speak with you. Remain here."

Steve did not resist. As Julius and Prince Arminius gathered the rest of their party, he looked around in the trees at the edge of the village. Night had fallen, leaving the forest too dark for him to see much, except in the dim, flickering torchlight that reached that far.

"I wish Hunter was here," Steve muttered.

Vicinius said nothing, but he released Steve's arm.

Together, they watched the visitors leave the village. Even after they had left, the warriors of the village remained gathered, talking excitedly among themselves.

"The time for action is coming," said Vicinius quietly. "Coming soon."

Steve nodded. "And MC 3 is still out there."

Wayne spent the early evening watching in a mixture of relief and amazement as Ishihara made a small lean-to. Ishihara used only fallen logs and dead branches, carefully avoiding damage to any living plants. When he had finished the shelter, he gathered deadwood and made a small fire.

By the softly crackling fire, Wayne ate more of his packaged food and then bundled up under the lean-to for the night. Ishihara sat against a tree trunk, ready to tend the fire through the night. With the fire for warmth and the robot standing guard, Wayne slept very well.

In the morning, Wayne ate while Ishihara carefully took apart the lean-to and scattered the pieces around the forest floor. Wayne felt that the precaution was not necessary, but he did not bother to argue. He was just glad to have Ishihara's help.

"What is our plan today?" Ishihara asked.

"We're going to hang out by that village again, remember? And look for MC 3."

"All right. As soon as I put out the fire completely, we can go."

Wayne got to his feet and looked up at the sky. It was still gray, of course, but no rain was falling. If he was lucky, they would grab MC 3 that day, before the weather turned worse, and they could go home.

At first light, the Roman bugler woke the entire Roman camp, including Gene and Jane. As the legionaries began to bustle with activity, Hunter waited outside the tent for Gene and Jane to rise and dress. As before, the sky was gray and the air moist and damp, but no rain was falling. Gene joined him; Jane left the tent and hurried toward the latrine. No Romans were nearby.

"I am going to search for Steve alone today, after all," said Hunter.

"What?" Gene looked at him in surprise. "I thought you didn't want to shuttle back and forth between us and Steve anymore. Look, Jane and I can be ready to go pretty quickly. We just need some breakfast and that won't take long. We won't slow you down."

"I considered this problem during the night," said Hunter. "I feel that both of you will be safest with the Romans until shortly before the actual ambush. You told me you cannot give me the date of the battle, but can you estimate if it is imminent?"

"Well, maybe this will help," said Gene slowly. "The German ambush took place when the Roman troops were moving through a rugged mountain pass. It was between the Weser River, which is visible down the slope right below us, and the sites of some German cities that don't exist yet. I would say we're getting pretty close to the spot."

"That may help." Hunter reviewed the terrain he had seen the previous day in the direction that the Romans would travel after breaking camp. "I do not believe any mountain passes are within today's marching distance."

"Then it won't happen today."

"All right. That is good. I shall go straight to Vicinius's village this morning, since I left him with Steve out in the forest yesterday."

"What should we do? We can meet you out there someplace if you want."

"No, we shall lose track of each other again," said Hunter. "I shall bring him back to the Roman army for tonight, meeting you wherever I can on the march. Tomorrow morning, when we are all together again, we can leave the Romans in time to avoid the battle."

"Okay." Gene shrugged.

"Tell Jane the current plan," said Hunter. "I should begin my journey."

"Got it."

Hunter did not bother requesting a horse, since that might cause another minor historical change; his team had risked enough of those. Besides, he could reach the village on foot soon enough for his purpose. The question of whether Marcus would still decide to burn a village because of Hunter's team had sharpened his concern over small changes starting larger ones.

The sentries at the gate opened it for Hunter as he approached. He merely nodded his thanks and slipped out into the forest again. If he could reach

Steve by midday, as he expected, then he could at least have his team together again by night. As the battle approached, he was determined to have his team together where he could keep them safe. MC 3 could wait until they were reunited.

Marcus arranged for Gene and Jane to ride with him at the head of the Roman column with Governor Varus. This was a little unusual for guests, but the governor said nothing about it. Marcus had come to feel responsible for them. On the march, he rode on the governor's right, with Jane and Gene to the right of him.

Advance patrols were riding out, as usual, to check the road. Marcus had asked them to take special pains in looking for signs of hostility, but he had not succeeded in convincing them that the governor was overconfident, either. Besides, as an aide to the governor, he had prestige but no direct authority in their chain of command.

When the column halted for its midday meal and a rest, Marcus reined in and looked out across the country ahead before dismounting. "Well, it could be worse, I guess."

"What do you see?" Jane asked.

Marcus pointed into the distance. "For the rest of today, the road skirts the edge of this mountain, high upon the slope. And the ground above us is fairly clear—it only has some scrub trees and open meadows. No one can hide up there to attack us. If they come across that area from somewhere else, we'll have plenty of warning."

Governor Varus had already dismounted and handed

his reins to a groom, but he looked up with a weary smile. "Tribune, I'm glad you feel safer now than you did this morning." Shaking his head, he walked away.

Marcus sighed and dismounted as well. Then he saw one of the advance patrols returning to the column, where they would report to the centurion who was their immediate superior. "Excuse me a moment, will you?"

"Of course," said Jane, jumping to the ground. "I'll take a little walk."

"I'll just relax right here," said Gene. "And try not to get in the way."

Marcus picked his way through the crowd of legionaries and horses to the advance patrol. They had dismounted and were holding their horses impatiently, anxious to be dismissed. The commander of the patrol, a man named Adrianus, was breathlessly giving his report. Marcus approached them to listen.

" . . . so many villages in the area that are empty," Adrianus was saying.

"What?" Marcus interrupted. "Excuse me, centurion, but I want to hear this, too. Adrianus, you say that some German villages are completely empty?"

The centurion, a man named Fabius Albinus, waited patiently. Marcus was glad; the centurion would be within his rights to tell the governor's aide to go away. Of course, at some point in the future, he could find that annoying the governor's aide unnecessarily had been a mistake.

"Uh—no, sir, I didn't mean they were totally empty," said Adrianus. "I just meant, they're empty of all their fighting men."

"How many villages?"

"Every village we passed, sir. All day."

"But the women, children, and old men were still there?" Marcus asked.

"Yes, sir."

"Did you ask them where the men were?"

"Yes, sir. They said, out in the fields or out hunting." Adrianus glanced at his men, behind him, some of whom nodded agreement.

"Did you go past their fields?"

"Of course we did. The harvest is past. All the fields are deserted."

"You don't think they're hunting, Tribune?" Fabius looked at Marcus. "Game has been plentiful; it would tempt a man to go out after it."

"Too many men are missing all at once just to be hunting," said Marcus. "Game *has* been plentiful; a major hunt with many men at one time is unnecessary."

"Excuse me, sir—we saw some of the men," said Adrianus. "Here and there."

"Where?" Marcus demanded. "Doing what?"

"Avoiding us, mostly. They slipped away into the woods pretty fast when they saw us. But they were generally headed that way." He pointed up ahead.

"On our line of march?" Marcus asked, looking where he was pointing.

"Well—not along the road." Adrianus frowned thoughtfully. "From what we could see, they were going overland. But their route could intersect ours, I guess."

"They're traveling overland through the forest to avoid being seen if possible," said Marcus. "And even though you spotted some of them, I doubt you saw any more than the smallest fraction. Adrianus, what do you make of it?"

"Uh . . ." Adrianus glanced uncomfortably at his immediate superior, aware that the army's formal position was that no danger was present.

"Speak freely," said Marcus, eyeing the centurion pointedly. "I want to hear your opinion."

"Well, something is up, sir. Looks to me like they're planning a fight."

"I think so, too," said Marcus. "Arminius is making his move." He turned and strode away, leaving Adrianus to complete his report to Fabius.

The real danger now, Marcus told himself, was not from the Germans. They were poorly armed, poorly armored, and generally undisciplined on the battlefield. The danger was in the attitude of Governor Varus, who was being reckless enough to invite disaster despite the many advantages that the Roman army possessed.

This time, Marcus did not simply want to run up to the governor like a panicked new recruit. He had apparently lost some of Governor Varus's respect already over this matter. Instead, he would have to maintain his dignity and try to approach the subject casually.

Marcus joined Governor Varus at his cookfire, where Demetrius had prepared their noonday meal. Jane and Gene were just sitting down on a couple of large rocks there as well, accepting plates of beans fried in bacon grease. It was normal marching fare, quick and easy to prepare.

"I don't like the look of those foul clouds," said Governor Varus, glancing up. "Or the way the wind is coming up. We've had a short reprieve these last few days from the infernal rain. Now I would say we'll get another downpour tonight or tomorrow. What do you think, Marcus?"

Marcus took his plate from Demetrius and looked up. "Yes, Governor. I think a storm is building. The winds through these mountains are unpredictable, though. I would say, it will hit us tomorrow."

Governor Varus nodded, chewing, then swallowed. "Gene, what do you think?"

"Uh—we don't have mountains like this where I'm from," said Gene. "But it looks like rain again soon."

Governor Varus nodded. "Marcus, I hope I have not been too hard on you about these Germans."

"Well, sir—I know I haven't been here as long as you have. One of our patrols returned just now with some information, however."

"Mm?" The governor's mouth was full.

"They found that the fighting men have left the villages." Instead of pressing his argument, Marcus paused to eat for a moment.

Jane and Gene looked at each other.

"I wouldn't worry," Governor Varus said to them. "They're probably out hunting."

"Our patrol spotted some of them," said Marcus. "They were sneaking through the forest overland, off the road, moving up ahead of us."

"Maybe they have good hunting grounds that way," said Jane. Her voice was quiet, oddly timid.

"Oh, I suppose there may be some troublemakers among them," said Governor Varus. "All of Rome's many subject peoples get restless from time to time. That doesn't mean they can mount a serious rebellion."

"It might be worth checking out," said Marcus, looking at the governor hopefully.

"Our patrols should be sufficient," said Governor Varus. "After all, they brought back this information. They can handle it."

"It wouldn't hurt—" Marcus began.

"No, no. You see, this province is virtually an extension of Gaul." The Governor turned to Gene. "How long has Gaul been conquered, now?"

"About half a century," said Gene.

"And have you seen any objection to Roman rule there in your lifetime?"

"Well, no. I haven't." He smiled slightly.

"The Germans are also subjugated," said Governor Varus. "I expect in a few years we will be ready to press eastward, to conquer the land beyond the Elbe River." He shrugged, and continued eating.

"May I have the commander of the patrol report directly to you, sir?" Marcus asked. "Maybe if—"

"No!" Governor Varus tossed aside his empty plate and stood up. "Tribune, I have tired of this subject. Do not bring me any officer. Do not argue with me any further. You are expressly forbidden from discussing any changes in marching orders with regular officers or interfering with existing army directives of any kind in *any* way. And *if* you have any questions for the Germans, you may ask them tonight! The matter is closed!" He waved a hand in dismissal.

Marcus stood up, his appetite gone. As Demetrius began cleaning up, Marcus turned to Gene and Jane. "What do you think? Based on what you heard?"

"Uh—" Caught off guard, Gene looked at Jane and shrugged. "Well . . . I'm a trader, not a soldier."

"I'm not asking you as a soldier," said Marcus. "Just as someone who has overheard what I told the governor. What do you think?"

"I think," Jane said slowly, "that the governor should respect your opinions more."

Marcus was startled. "Well—thank you. But do you think I'm being reckless?"

"Did the men in the advance patrol share your opinion?" Gene asked.

"Yes, at least their field commander did. His superior didn't."

"I'm sure you know your business," Gene said carefully. "I'm sorry you can't get the governor to listen to you."

"Me, too," said Jane, with a tight little smile.

Marcus nodded. "Well . . . thank you for the thought. It's time to mount up."

"What did he mean about asking the Germans questions tonight?" Jane asked.

Marcus took his reins from the groom. "It means that we are feasting with some of their leaders tonight, in camp. Probably Prince Arminius himself, among others." He shook his head in disgust and mounted.

When Steve rose the next morning, he kept close to Vicinius and said very little. The village was in a war-like mood; even early in the morning, the warriors sat by the cookfires tending their weapons, scraping the shafts of their spears smooth and sharpening their knives and their few swords on rocks. Steve could do nothing at this stage but wait for Hunter to come back for him.

As the morning wore on, Steve still sat by the fire near Vicinius's hut, watching the groups of warriors. After Steve finished eating, he still did not want to risk doing anything that would attract attention to himself. Chief Odover walked among the warriors, talking quietly and nodding approval when they showed him their weapons.

Vicinius spoke to them for a while, but then returned to his fire. He sat down with Steve and he used a small stone to sharpen his spear point. No one else came near them.

"Are you going to war today?" Steve asked quietly,

watching Vicinius patiently slide the stone across the metal with a regular, steady motion.

"Today or tonight, I think," said Vicinius. "My father told me a little while ago that Prince Arminius will send someone to get us. He is feasting with the Romans tonight."

"He is?"

"You may remain here, of course. It is not your fight."

Suddenly a chorus of shouts arose from the far side of the village. When Steve looked up, he saw the warriors crowding around Hunter as he emerged from the trees, his head and shoulders visible over the shorter Germans. The warriors were shouting angrily at him.

"Hey!" Vicinius leaped up and ran toward them. "Hunter is my guest here, remember?"

Steve hesitated, watching the others. Then he decided that staying close to Hunter was a good idea. He walked forward slowly, following Vicinius.

The warriors were dragging Hunter forward now, shouting at him. Steve knew that Hunter could pull away from them if he wanted, but he would not leave Steve alone in a hostile atmosphere. Finally the warriors shoved Hunter toward Vicinius.

"Your friends are spies!" One of the warriors pointed angrily at Vicinius.

"Watch your tongue, Sigismund," said Vicinius, standing with Hunter in front of Steve.

"He came from the direction of the Roman camp!" Sigismund jabbed his spear point into the ground. "Some of us were out looking for more branches to use as spear shafts, and we saw him coming!"

Most of the warriors began yelling again, but Odover approached them and stood quietly between Vicinius and Sigismund. Everyone quieted, waiting to see what the village chief would say. He turned to Hunter.

"The question is a good one," said Odover patiently. "Tell us where you spent the night. Were you with the Romans?"

"I was," said Hunter.

The warriors began yelling again, but Odover held up his hand for silence. He got it.

"You have been our guest here. What have you told the Romans of us?"

"I told them I am still searching for all the members of my party," said Hunter. "I wish to return home to safety with them, nothing more."

"He lies," Sigismund growled.

"Test him," Steve said suddenly. "See what he'll tell you about them, instead." Since the Germans were clearly about to mount their attack, and were supposed to defeat the Romans anyway, Steve figured that helping them a little would be acceptable. Besides, Hunter could be trusted to judge for himself what to reveal.

"Speak, Hunter," Odover said quietly.

"Tell us their line of march," said Sigismund, glaring at Hunter.

"They march along the road that overlooks the Weser River," said Hunter. "Today, it will take them high on the shoulder of a mountain overlooking the river, with open country above it. Tomorrow the country becomes more rugged, and they will have to choose between a couple of different passes through the mountains."

"That is right," said Sigismund slowly. "From what I have heard."

"Prince Arminius knows his business," said Hunter. "All we ask is to go in peace and gather our party together."

"Keep them here," said Sigismund. "Until the action has begun."

"No," said Vicinius. "They will not be prisoners here. I brought them here as my guests and they will go in peace." He turned to Hunter and nodded.

"Steve." Hunter inclined his head toward the forest and began to walk that way.

Steve glanced at Vicinius, who was shifting his position to remain between Sigismund and Hunter. Then Steve trotted toward the edge of the village, paralleling Hunter so he would not have to pass any of the hostile warriors. As soon as he reached the trees, he slowed down to pick his way through the underbrush to Hunter.

Suddenly shouts rose up behind him. When he turned to look, he saw Sigismund shove Vicinius aside and lead the warriors after Hunter and him, shaking their weapons. Steve took off at a run, crashing through the bushes and dodging around trees.

"This way, Steve," Hunter called. He angled behind Steve, cutting off the warriors. "Run!"

"Like I didn't know better," Steve muttered, pausing to yank his cloak free of a branch.

The warriors were yelling at the edge of the village, but that was all they were doing. They were not throwing their spears or shooting arrows. Steve decided, as he shoved between a couple of large bushes, that they were merely helping their visitors on their way.

After a few minutes, Steve stopped to catch his breath. The village was already out of sight. Hunter joined him.

"You are well?" Hunter asked.

"Yeah, I'm fine. Now what?"

"We shall spend the night with Jane and Gene in the Roman camp. Tomorrow, I believe, the attack will take place. We shall leave the Romans tomorrow morning and avoid the violence."

"Sounds good to me." Steve looked up at the sky. Through the canopy of trees and the dark clouds, he could see only a hint of the sun's position. "But it's only late morning now, isn't it? We have the rest of the day. You want to go back to the Romans already?"

"We must not let them get too far from us," said Hunter. "Because of the heavy wagons in their baggage train, and the time they require to prepare in the morning and to make camp at night, they will move more slowly than we shall. However, since we are both on foot, our advantage is not too great."

"From everything I've heard, MC 3 may be over at a neighboring village. At least, they know something about him. I think we ought to take a look."

"I agree," said Hunter. "We should try to avoid both German warriors who may be moving and also any Roman patrols. At this stage, both sides are becoming wary of strangers."

"It's okay with me. But, I don't know if I can find this other village."

"There are many trails through the forest. I know which general direction to take. We shall find it."

Steve had little to say as Hunter chose a direction and led him through the trees. Asking him how he was making his choices would invite an answer that was more complicated than it was worth. Between the data about the terrain and the forest that Hunter had stored continuously since arriving, and his enhanced hearing, Hunter was using too much information that he would have to explain at length. Steve decided just to keep walking.

Hunter located a trail fairly quickly but they left it periodically to avoid Germans Hunter heard coming. Some were warriors walking with a quiet determination. Others were old men simply out gathering firewood. When the Germans had passed, Hunter returned to the trail.

On several occasions, he mentioned to Steve that he could hear small groups of horses in the distance. They were almost certainly Roman patrols, but they never drew near enough to alter Hunter's direction. Hunter and Steve spent several hours moving through the forest, sometimes retracing their steps and moving from one trail to another.

Wayne spent much of the day hiding outside the village of Prince Arminius. Ishihara was adept at moving them to remain upwind of the village dogs and to avoid the war parties that kept arriving in the village. Prince Arminius received each war party enthusiastically. Then he sent them on their way, always in the same direction. Julius remained near him, and MC 3 stayed close to Julius.

"Julius must have said something to him about helping him or not straying too far," said Wayne. "MC

3 has to be responding to a Second Law instruction to behave so consistently."

"Very likely," said Ishihara.

"When they found me here, they tied me up. Yet they seem to have adopted him."

"Perhaps his willingness to cooperate under the Second Law made him seem like a friend," said Ishihara.

"Yeah, maybe. He must have shown up as a kind of lost crazy man. But it's all going to make getting him away harder. If he won't leave Julius's side, we'll have to hope Julius and MC 3 go take a few minutes away from everyone else."

"I have observed Julius's trip to the latrine in the hope that they would be alone," said Ishihara. "However, with so many visiting warriors, that has not been the case."

"You have any suggestions?" Wayne asked sourly.

"Only to wait for our opportunity," said Ishihara. "Impatience would be a mistake."

"I was afraid you'd say that."

Marcus did not speak to the Governor as they rode side by side at the head of the army during the afternoon. Occasionally he made a few friendly observations to Jane about the weather or the scenery. Actually, however, he was carefully eyeing the muddy road ahead as they topped every rise and rounded every curve.

He did not expect German warriors to appear unannounced on the open slopes that the army was crossing that day. What he was looking for was rugged, difficult terrain in the distance that they would have to cross the next day or the day after that. Late in the afternoon, when the army halted to make camp, he remained mounted and examined the winding route that lay in front of them.

"What is it, Marcus?" Jane looked from the road back to him. "You see something?"

"Nothing dangerous at this moment," said Marcus. "But do you see how the road forks, down this slope in the distance?"

Jane paused, looking. Finally she nodded. "Oh, I see it, now. The army will reach that fork in the first hour of marching tomorrow."

"I'm not sure which way we're going. But the fork on the left leads into some very rugged country."

Governor Varus dismounted and glanced up at him. "Something wrong, Tribune?"

"No, sir. Uh—I thought I might take our guests on a brief ride back along the troops for a moment, though, if they're interested in seeing the sights."

"You haven't had enough riding for the day?" Governor Varus shook his head, handed his reins to a groom, and wearily walked away.

"Would you come with me for a moment?" Marcus asked, looking at Jane and Gene.

"Sure." Gene shrugged.

"Lead on," said Jane.

Marcus steered them around to the side of the column, which was dispersing to build the camp. He rode back to Fabius Albinus, the centurion in command of the advance patrols. Fabius had just dismounted, and was dismissing one of the patrols that had just returned and reported.

"Centurion," said Marcus, looking down at him.

"Have your patrols reported whether any German villages are close by?"

"Yes, sir, they have. Several are close."

"I have a favor to ask, Fabius." Marcus made his tone more casual, since he had no direct authority to give Fabius an order. "I'd like to see a few of them myself, but I don't dare go without a large escort."

"I can send a couple of decuries with you. Almost all the patrols have rejoined us now."

"I had more in mind, Fabius. Would you ride out with me—and bring your entire troop?"

"The entire century?"

"Would you mind? Perhaps for an hour, no more."

"The men have been riding all day. They're ready to stand down," Fabius said slowly.

Marcus merely waited, as Fabius studied his face. They both knew the time would come when Marcus could return the favor.

"All right, Marcus. I'll take them out with you."

"Thank you, Fabius. I won't forget it."

As Fabius mounted again and called out his orders, Jane moved up next to Marcus and leaned close to him.

"Marcus? Are you going to get into trouble over this with the governor?"

Surprised that she would question his decision, he almost ordered her to back away. Her tone of genuine concern stopped him, however. Next to her, Gene also was watching him. After all, they had heard the governor tell him earlier not to interfere with existing marching orders or army directives.

"It may be a problem," Marcus said quietly. "But if I can learn something that will convince the governor to stop a disaster, then this will be worth the risk."

"Please don't," said Jane.

"I'll be fine. But I must ask you two to remain in camp with Demetrius. I will be back soon."

Fabius had his century of cavalry mounted and in formation in only moments. He nodded to Marcus, who drew up next to him at the head of the column. Then Fabius spurred his mount to lead them out.

"Halt! Halt, I say!"

Marcus clenched his teeth at the sound of Governor Varus's voice. He forced himself to remain calm, however. On his left, the governor angrily strode across the mud toward him. Behind Governor Varus, Jane and Gene had dismounted but were watching.

"Centurion, dismiss your troop," said the governor. "Return to your normal duties."

"Governor Varus—" Fabius began.

"Don't waste your breath," Governor Varus growled. "The tribune doesn't need any excuses from you."

Fabius turned and began a quick stream of orders to his century.

"Get down, Marcus," ordered the governor.

"Governor, we need to know what the local villages—"

"Or you may lose your position, *Tribune*. Dismount!"

Marcus jumped to the ground.

"I have already heard all of your arguments. I will not listen to them again. Prince Arminius will be joining us at any time, with some members of his own party. I suggest you remain at my tent with your guests. Alert me the moment Prince Arminius arrives." Governor Varus turned and hurried away.

Marcus sighed. At least he was still a tribune. He took the reins of his horse and walked toward the governor's tent, which had been raised already.

Jane stood silently with Gene as Marcus led his horse past them and handed his reins to a groom. When Marcus had moved out of hearing, she turned to Gene and shrugged. They had heard the entire exchange between the governor and Marcus. Around them, the new camp was slowly going up.

"It was kind of a dirty trick, wasn't it?" Jane drew her cloak tighter around her.

"We had no choice," said Gene. "We had to point out Marcus's intentions to the governor. There was no other way to stop him and he might have discovered tomorrow's ambush if he had ridden out right now in strength."

"You're sure now that it's coming tomorrow?"

"Yeah." Gene nodded, looking at her grimly. "The governor said that Prince Arminius is coming tonight. The German entourage feasts with the Romans tonight—that means the attack is tomorrow."

"Then Hunter had better get back here tonight and

get us away from the Romans, as he planned."

"Exactly."

Late in the day Hunter and Steve were hidden in the forest outside the village. They had watched MC 3 following Julius around in the village as other warriors came and went. Then Prince Arminius had led a group of warriors out of the village, but Julius, MC 3, and most of the warriors from this village had remained.

When Prince Arminius had left, Hunter had raised his hearing to maximum sensitivity as a safety measure. Immediately after doing so, he had detected the presence of two figures also hidden in the brush nearby. He turned to Steve.

"We are not alone in observing this village. Two others are doing the same, roughly a hundred yards to our left, completely out of sight."

"Romans?"

"I doubt it. They have been relying on cavalry patrols for this kind of work."

"Then who is it?"

"I suspect that one is Wayne and the other probably a German warrior whom Wayne has somehow convinced to help him. Judging by their position and their lack of movement, they have not yet noticed our presence."

"Maybe we should grab Wayne," whispered Steve. "Get him out of our way once and for all."

"Doing so now would cause a disturbance," said Hunter. "It would reveal our presence and thereby our interest in observing this village."

"Hold it—you mean you're just going to let Wayne stay right here with his eye on MC 3 and *leave* him here? Hunter, that's crazy—even worse, irrational."

"I disagree. I see no way in which Wayne can rush into the village and grab MC 3. We know that MC 3 is surrounded by too many Germans, all of whom are looking for a fight."

Steve shook his head in disbelief. "Well, we still have to decide what we're going to do for the night. It's getting late now, anyway. If we're going to find the Roman camp tonight, we have to get moving. It's a long walk from here."

"Getting MC 3 now would endanger too many humans," said Hunter.

"He will resist and they will defend him. With that many opponents, I would not be able to get him away without harming them."

"At the very least, let's go sneak up on Wayne and get a good look at him—at least a positive identification. That way we'll know for sure."

"Yes, that is wise. I can make this approach more efficiently alone, however. Please remain here."

"Yeah, okay."

Hunter started to move when he received a signal on his internal receiver. "Hunter, Jane calling."

"Yes, Jane," Hunter radioed.

"The Romans are making camp again for the night," she said quietly. "We found out that Prince Arminius is bringing a party of Germans here for a feast. Gene says that means the attack will start tomorrow."

"Are you in danger now?"

"No. We're fine. But I can't talk long. We're in the middle of camp. Gene and I are huddled together pretending to talk to each other."

"Does Gene anticipate danger tonight?"

"I'm here, Hunter," said Gene. "No, I don't. We just wanted to make sure you were kept up-to-date."

"Hunter?" Steve looked at him. "Something wrong?"

"I have a call from Jane and Gene," Hunter said aloud. "Please wait."

"Should we still follow the original plan?" Gene asked. "Are you rejoining us here tonight or should we try to meet you somewhere?"

"Steve is with me now," said Hunter. "Remain where you are. We shall come back to the Roman camp tonight and reunite the team, as planned. Hunter out."

Steve was still watching Hunter curiously.

"We shall go to the new Roman camp now," said Hunter. "The attack will begin tomorrow."

"Wait a minute." Steve's eyes widened. "You mean we're going to leave MC 3 right here? We almost have him. We could grab him and take him back to our time—then come back for Jane and Gene."

"I do not dare take the risk," said Hunter. "I still feel that we are not very close to apprehending MC 3. The fact that we have been able to see him does not imply that we can simply grab him and run."

"But he's the entire reason we're here. Isn't taking the opportunity worth the risk?"

"I must balance the risk to harm of our future with the danger of harm to the individual warriors and to you. Remember, some of the Germans in the village may play an important role in the battle. If I injure them, I could also alter our future. Nor can I risk harm to you unnecessarily."

"Well . . ." Steve shook his head. "I can't think of an argument against that. But I hate walking away from MC 3 when he's so close."

"I believe that Julius will join the attack and that MC 3 will go with him. We will know where to find him."

"Yeah, all right. I guess." Steve shrugged.

"In any case, if we get MC 3 in custody while the team is together, we can leave immediately. That is the most desirable plan of action."

"You're the boss."

Hunter listened carefully for signs of movement in the two strangers but heard nothing. The wind had not changed, so they were still upwind of the village dogs. He turned and slipped through the trees once more, with Steve behind him.

Steve was exhausted by the time they reached the new Roman camp. Night had fallen, but the sky over the palisade fence was brightly lighted by the flickering glow of many fires. The sentries saw them coming and when Hunter merely waved, they opened the front gate.

Inside, Steve saw why the sentries were in a friendly mood. A feast was well under way, with boars and deer roasting on spits all over the camp. The soldiers were talking and drinking; around some of the fires, groups were singing.

Outside the governor's tent, a tight ring of torches on tall posts surrounded the main party. They were seated on logs around a boar roasting over a roaring fire. In the light thrown by the fire, Steve could see Governor Varus, some soldiers he guessed were top officers of the army, and a large group of bearded German guests dressed in heavy furs.

"Do you see Jane and Gene anywhere?" Steve asked. "Or Marcus?"

"Yes," said Hunter. "Marcus is seated behind the governor. Jane and Gene are sitting with him. We should walk around the outside of the circle to the far side."

"Whatever you say."

Steve followed Hunter on a long route through the crowds of festive legionaries. Jane saw them coming first and waved. Marcus and Gene greeted them when they arrived, but the tribune did not bother to tell the governor about their arrival.

Hunter and Steve sat next to Gene, on the far side from Marcus. In the row ahead of them, Steve could see Prince Arminius sitting next to Governor Varus. The German on the other side of Prince Arminius was a little shorter, an older man with long steel gray hair and a lined face.

"Gene?" Steve leaned close to him. "Any idea who the old guy is? All the other Germans here are of warrior age."

"I know who he is, all right. His name is Segestes. He's Prince Arminius's father."

"Really?" Hunter asked. "Why is he not the Prince of the Cherusci, then?"

"Arminius was elected chief of the Cherusci," said Gene. "He commanded a troop of German auxiliaries in the Roman army a few years ago and was elected chief after he quit that position. And Segestes has had considerable friction with his son." Gene glanced over at them to make sure no one outside the team, including Marcus, was listening.

"What is wrong?" Hunter asked.

Gene lowered his voice. "Sometime tonight, Segestes will get Varus alone and betray Arminius's plan to rebel tomorrow. But he can't convince the governor any more than Marcus has been able to."

"It's hard to believe Governor Varus is so hard-headed," Jane whispered. "He has all these warnings and all the evidence around him, if he only would look at it."

"We must be glad he does not change his mind," Hunter reminded her.

"History is full of people who were blind like that," said Gene. "Many historical figures seem incredibly blind, ignorant, or stupid in their actions, but of course we have the advantage of hindsight."

"Yeah, he's overconfident," said Steve. "I guess when you look at how well armed and organized the Romans are, and then look at the furs and the few weapons the Germans have, it's understandable."

"Discontinue this line of talk," said Hunter. "We are taking a reckless chance of being overheard. Save it for when we are alone, preferably back home."

Soon the boar on the spit in front of the governor was fully roasted, at least on the outside. Roman slaves carved off chunks of it; Demetrius served them with plenty of wine and freshly baked bread. Meanwhile, the remainder of the boar still roasted over the fire.

Steve eagerly accepted his dinner. The meat was tough and greasy, but he was too hungry to care. Conversation stopped while the team ate.

After a while, Marcus set his plate down on the ground, with food still on it. He picked up his wine goblet and stood up, studying the Germans in the front row by the fire. Jane looked up at him curiously.

"I think I will mingle with our guests," he said grimly. Then, forcing a tight smile, he moved up to the front row of seats and began talking to some of the visitors.

"I am reconsidering our plan," said Hunter.

"Huh?" Gene looked up. "You don't want to stay with the Romans for the battle tomorrow, do you?"

"Not at all," said Hunter. "Now that we are together, I think perhaps we should leave the camp tonight. I can make camp somewhere not too far from here and stand guard over you while you sleep."

"Why the change in plans?" Steve asked. "Why don't we just take off tomorrow morning?"

"Marcus may force us to remain with him tomorrow for our own safety. I do not want to risk that."

"I don't think Marcus will be too happy about our going tonight, either," said Gene. "He'll think it's too dangerous to leave now, too."

"We shall not discuss it with Marcus or anyone else," said Hunter. "For now, we shall participate in the feast as guests. Maybe when the Germans leave, we shall be able to slip out in the confusion. If not, I shall look for another opportunity later tonight."

Steve turned away. In front of him, Prince Arminius was raising his goblet to Governor Varus. Curious, Steve leaned forward slightly to listen.

"You have been a great help to me," said Governor Varus, clanking his goblet against his companion's. "You warned me that this expedition was necessary to keep the tribes docile. And without your advice about the necessity of gathering winter provisions, I would never have sent so many troops out to different parts of the province to prepare for winter."

"I'm glad to be of service, Governor." Prince Arminius took a drink of his wine.

"I will tell you plainly, I look forward to returning to our forts on the Rhine. This rainy season of yours is very cold and gray."

"Perhaps I can help you in this matter, as well, Governor Varus."

"Eh? How so?"

"The road you follow takes a long route through the mountains. I can direct you through some mountain passes that will shorten the distance you will have to travel."

"Really?" Governor Varus sipped his wine again. "On which day we will reach these passes?"

"Tomorrow," said Prince Arminius. "Before we leave you this evening for our own camp, I will tell you how to go."

"Ah! I thank you again, Arminius."

Steve glanced over at Marcus. The tribune was gazing into the fire, too far away to have overheard the conversation. Then Steve turned to Hunter, who simply nodded with satisfaction.

Late that night, the fires finally died down. Most of the legionaries had gone to sleep when Steve watched the governor and his party, including Marcus, escort their German guests to the gate of the camp. This elite party of Germans, unlike the bulk of German warriors, was mounted, and they rode out into the night with torches to light their way.

Hunter stood up and casually walked away from the fire. Steve saw that Jane and Gene followed him and hurried after them. No one else took any notice of them. Hunter stopped by a deserted spot against the back wall of the palisade, where they would not be overheard by any of the Romans.

"Most of the camp will be asleep soon," said Hunter. "When only the sentries are awake, we shall leave the camp. I want to discuss the plan with you now, so we shall not have to talk very much when the time comes."

"Are we going to sneak out the gate?" Steve asked. "Those sentries probably had some wine, too. Maybe they'll doze off in a little while."

"I believe that is too risky," said Hunter. "Since it is their duty to remain on guard, I do not wish to count on their failing to do so. Maybe they will remain alert. Opening the main gate will make some noise and, of course, torches are lighting the area. If they do interrupt us, I cannot risk harming them, as you know, to facilitate our escape."

"Okay, okay," muttered Steve. "What about creating a diversion? We could let a small fire spread or let some of the horses loose in a spot where the sentries will have to deal with the problem. Then we could sneak out."

"I fear a move such as that could get out of hand," said Hunter.

"What are we going to do, then?" Jane asked.

"We shall have to go over the wall. For now, please follow your normal evening routine. Go into the tent as though you are retiring for the night, but remain dressed. I shall walk around the camp and find the right place to go. When I come for you, we shall leave."

Wayne huddled in the forest, stiff with the cold, as he and Ishihara kept watch outside the village of Prince Arminius. He could not build a fire this close to the village, of course, without being noticed. Yet hardly anyone in the village had gone to sleep there either.

"These German war parties were arriving all evening," said Ishihara. "But now we have not seen a new one for several hours. I believe that all the parties who are coming have probably passed through this village by now."

"They must have come from villages all over the area," said Wayne. "I wonder where they're going."

"Julius is still here with his companions," said Ishihara. "So MC 3 is still here, too."

"Look, if they do go to sleep, can you sneak into the village to grab MC 3 again? Now that I'm here, you don't have to run away with him. All you have to do is come back out here to me and I'll take us back home again."

"Once the villagers are asleep, I can make another attempt," said Ishihara. "However, I must inform you that I believe MC 3 will be even more alert than ever to the sound of my approach. His hearing will be highly sensitized for my footsteps. Combined with the presence of his friends, we may find that apprehending him the same way—"

"Hey, now what?" Wayne pointed through the brush toward the village. "Look."

The last group of warriors, the men of this village, were finally moving out. Julius was leading the way, with MC 3 right behind him. Many of them carried torches that revealed their direction as they slipped into the forest on the far side of the village.

"They must be joining the others," said Ishihara. "I suggest we follow MC 3 as best we can, from a safe distance. What is your instruction?"

"Yeah, good idea." Wayne sighed. Maybe the activity would warm him up. "You lead."

Hunter walked quietly through the camp after the rest of the team went into their tent. He wanted to leave the camp without attracting the notice of the Romans. Occasionally, when he became aware that a sentry or slave on cleanup duty had noticed him, he would pause by one of the spits to taste another piece of roasted meat or to warm his hands by the dying embers. Gradually, they lost interest in him as they performed their duties. Almost everyone in the camp was asleep now.

Finally, near the horse corral, Hunter found a spot in the palisade wall that suited his purpose. The baggage wagons were lined up in precise rows near the corral. The wagons blocked the view of the grooms, who were sleeping around a fire close by, so they could not see him if they awoke. The horses obstructed the view of the sentries at the main gate. Even better, a few of the horses were awake, snorting and walking around to take a look at him.

The sounds the horses made would help disguise any noise the team made getting over the wall. Hunter saw that the ropes used with the horses were carefully coiled nearby. He would need to borrow some ropes, but he would return them. This was the place for them to go over the wall unnoticed.

Hunter patiently picked his way back to the tent where the human members of his team were waiting, still stopping occasionally to look up at the starless sky or at a dwindling fire. No one challenged him. At the entrance of the tent, he merely leaned inside.

"Are you ready?" Hunter asked quietly.

Without a word, Steve, Gene, and Jane got up and followed him. Once again, he played the little game of wandering, stopping, and idly looking around. He did see one of the sentries at the gate watching them for few moments, but then the sentry yawned and gazed in another direction for a while. Hunter's companions followed his lead in silence.

When they were finally out of sight near the corral, Hunter uncoiled a rope and gauged its length. The palisade wall was about ten feet high, constructed of hastily cut tree trunks stripped of branches. All had been sunk into the wet ground and then tightly lashed together by just a few ropes near the top. It was not meant as a long-term defense, of course, but merely as a barrier to help protect the army for the night. Even the tops of the posts were cut roughly, not honed to a sharp point.

Hunter tied a slipknot in one end of a rope and tossed it up high. The loop caught over the top of a post, held in place by the stub of a pruned branch. Hunter climbed up the rope hand over hand and sat on the top of the fence, balancing on the ends of a couple of posts. The perch was extremely precarious, but it would not damage him. He doubted that any of the humans could sit there for long without minor injury.

From this position, Hunter could not see the sentries, but he could see most of the grooms and legionaries sleeping nearby. None of them had noticed him up in this unexpected location. He untied the slipknot in the rope and replaced it with a large loop held by a fixed knot that would not tighten. Then he dropped it to Steve, who caught it.

No words were necessary. Jane stepped carefully into the loop and grabbed the rope at her shoulder level. Then Hunter carefully lifted her hand over hand to the top of the palisade. He helped her climb over it and then lowered her gently on the rope the same way. Gene came next and Steve last. When all three were standing safely on the ground outside the wall, Hunter untied the loop, coiled the rope neatly, and tossed it back down by the other ropes, where the grooms would find it in the morning. Then he jumped down to join the others.

"Where are we going now?" Jane asked.

"We must find the site of the upcoming battle," said Hunter. "Cautiously, of course."

"What?" She looked at him in surprise. "I thought you'd want to avoid it completely."

"No. We must avoid being with the Romans. However, Steve and I last saw MC 3 closely following Julius. They will be at the battle. We must not allow MC 3 to interfere with its outcome in any way."

"You really think he can?" Steve shook his head. "We're talking about one unarmed robot in the middle of a battle with, how many, thousands of armed men?" He turned to Gene for confirmation.

"Thousands," Gene agreed.

"I doubt he can change the course of this battle," said Hunter. "It was an overwhelming victory for one side. However, I must consider the possibility. If I can somehow apprehend MC 3 before or during the battle, I must do so. To keep you three from harm, I ask you to stay as safe as you can."

"Well, let's get going, then," said Steve.

Hunter reviewed his internal map, to which he had been adding information constantly during the time he had been here. He had seen which way the road went on the anticipated line of march, but even now that was too dangerous for them to take. He selected a route through the forest, partly on narrow forest trails that he had already seen. It would bring them to a slope that overlooked the valley where the ambush would take place.

"Come," said Hunter.

For the first hour or so, Hunter led his team alone through the darkness. The going was very slow even on the trails, since the overcast sky and the forest canopy allowed little moonlight to reach them. However, he saw flickering torchlight ahead shortly after the hour mark.

Knowing the torches were carried by German warriors, Hunter followed them at a safe distance and saw more torches as time passed. Soon the way to the site of the ambush was obvious. Hunter merely followed the German warriors who were still on their way to their rendezvous. In the darkness, humans were only shadowed figures, individually unrecognizable. Any of the German warriors who saw Hunter and his team assumed they were more Germans and did not bother to speak.

Hunter considered the stress he would experience during the battle. On their previous mission, to Jamaica in the 1600s, he had participated in shipboard attacks by pirates. He had avoided interfering with the course of history, but he had felt extreme pressure from the First Law to stop humans from harming each other. Only his concentrated focus on the long-term harm that would result from altering history had kept him from making a serious mistake.

If he could not apprehend MC 3 before the actual attack began, then he would once again have to withstand thousands of First Law imperatives on all sides. Of course, MC 3 would also experience these imperatives. He could probably not stop enough German warriors to save the Romans, but that was another reason for Hunter to find the component robot before Governor Varus led his legionaries into disaster.

"Gene," Jane said quietly, as they walked. "Do you know anything about what happened to Marcus in the battle? Or afterward?"

"No."

"Not at all?"

"I'm afraid not," said Gene. "I suppose it's possible that if I went back to the primary sources, I might find some slight reference to the governor's personal aide, but I doubt it. One young tribune just wasn't all that important in the large picture."

"Did any of the Romans survive?"

"Yes, a very few."

"You are fond of the tribune?" Hunter asked.

"Well . . . he's been very nice," said Jane. "And very concerned about us."

"He's still a Roman conqueror," Steve grimly. "He thinks it's right just to march out here and kill people to take over their country just because the Roman Empire has enough military power to do it."

"Coming here has made all these people seem real to me," said Gene. "That's the difference."

"Our last historian said something like that, too," said Jane. "I can feel it myself."

"It's tough to think of Marcus falling in battle tomorrow," said Gene. "He's been very conscientious. And he's tried so hard to wake up Governor Varus to what's happening."

"I just hate to think of him having to die so young because the governor is an arrogant, overconfident idiot," said Jane. "It's so sad."

"He *could* make it," said Gene. "A very small number escape the battle and eventually reach the safety of the Rhine. But I can't swear to you that Marcus is among them."

"I understand your concern," said Hunter. "Please remember that none of us can act on it. Marcus must not be warned or aided in any way."

"He's on his own," Steve agreed.

Hunter followed the German warriors as they hiked along the side of an uneven slope. Finally, they all reached their places for the ambush. Hunter stopped to get his bearings as well as he could.

In the darkness, he was not able to see how far down the slope the valley floor lay, but he could hear the German warriors who were hidden all over the slope. Some talked quietly, but most breathed with the even rhythms of sleep. Hunter did not want to remain very close to any of them, since the arrival of daylight would reveal the presence of strangers among them. He changed direction and began to lead his team over the rocks and brush down the slope.

When Hunter's hearing told him that no German warriors were below him on the slope, he stopped and picked up a pebble. It was too small to harm any human if he tossed it lightly. He threw it forward, underhand, in a long, high arc. Then he waited for the sound of its landing.

The pebble struck faintly about forty-four meters away. Hunter picked up another pebble and threw it farther. This one landed approximately fifty-two meters away, but not much farther down than the first one. He picked up four more pebbles and threw them into the darkness, as well. Hunter was not able to reach a precise conclusion about the position of the valley floor from the places where they landed, but he estimated that the slope was leveling quickly.

"We shall find hiding places here," he said quietly. "Since the Germans have built no fires, we cannot either. Bundle up in your cloaks and rest as much as you can."

"Then what?" Jane came up next to him. "What are we going to do next?"

"We shall rise at dawn, to make sure we are prepared when the Romans march down the road. When I can see where we are in relation to the road and the Germans, I shall devise a more specific plan. It will take the Romans some time to form their march and actually arrive here."

"Good enough," said Steve. He elbowed Hunter playfully. "Say, Hunter. When we started hunting these component robots, I was the one arguing for improvisation all the time. You're doing more of it all the time."

"I am learning," said Hunter. "As you have indicated in the past, some situational challenges simply offer too many unpredictable variables to allow for rigid advance planning."

Steve laughed. "I don't think I phrased it exactly that way, but—yeah, that's right."

As the humans found comfortable spots to recline on the damp soil, Hunter stood over them, listening for any sound indicating that German warriors were coming toward them. He heard nothing. While they slept, however, he sat down and remained alert.

Wayne lay huddled on the slope, excited and also scared. He and Ishihara had followed Julius, MC 3, and their war party through the forest to the ambush site. As soon as Julius had selected a spot for the night, far down the slope toward the road, his party had doused their torches.

"Let's get him now," said Wayne.

"The risk to you is too great," said Ishihara. "We are surrounded by thousands of German warriors at this moment. Our best chance to apprehend MC 3 is during the confusion of battle. He will be distracted by the many First Law imperatives around him."

"So will you," said Wayne.

"The Germans will be even more distracted once the action begins," said Ishihara. "Neither they nor MC 3 will anticipate our approach from behind. That will give us the advantage we have lacked up to now."

"All right, all right. I don't want to get hurt, myself. In fact, I instruct you once again to focus on the necessity of getting me out of here safely once we grab MC 3. We don't have to go anywhere with him; I'll trigger my remote control right away and we'll take him right back to our own time, straight from the battlefield."

"I shall maintain this focus to the best of my ability," said Ishihara.

Steve used the leather bag as a pillow and dozed on the hard ground, waking frequently. His fur cloak and tunic kept him warm enough, but he could not get comfortable. The first light of morning woke him even before Hunter shook Jane and Gene gently.

Stiff from the poor rest, Steve pushed himself up and shivered when the cold wind whipped under his cloak. The early sunlight revealed heavy, dark clouds moving quickly. He could smell rain.

The road along the valley floor was close, about twenty-five meters down the slope. Steve looked around and saw thousands of German warriors all over the slope, among the boulders and trees, and even more across the narrow valley on the opposite slope. Others would be hidden from view. Of course, they were just waking; when the first sign of the Roman advance arrived, they would all slip out of sight.

To his relief, he did not see anyone from Vicinius's village nearby. Since everyone in Hunter's team was wearing German cloaks, they would not stand out to any of the other Germans. Steve relaxed a little.

Hunter was looking around the slopes, as well. "Gene, how does the battle proceed?"

"Uh—didn't we talk about this, already? It's a total rout for the Germans, who have brought a bunch of different tribes here—not just the Cherusci. The Romans were slaughtered and driven back to the Rhine forever. In fact, the Roman authorities thought the Germans might even invade Gaul."

"I have that in my data," Hunter said patiently. "What I mean is, what is the sequence of detailed events?"

"Oh—sorry." Gene shook his head. "It's hardly a battle at all. The Romans are trapped down on the road below us. Just as the attack begins, a huge thunderstorm hits."

"It's building already," said Jane, holding her cloak tight around her as she looked up at the sky.

"The well-disciplined Romans keep their position today and make camp for the night, totally surrounded. Then at sunrise tomorrow—"

"I understand," said Hunter. "That is what I need for now."

"What do you want us to do?" Jane asked.

"Steve, do you still have some cold food in your bag?" Hunter asked.

"Yeah."

"Distribute it. I want all of you to be as well fed as possible. You must hide and remain together when the action begins."

Steve pulled open the bag and took out some of the roasted meat that was still wrapped in leaves. In the cold weather, it was still good. He passed some to Jane and Gene. "We don't have any water. When it starts to rain, open your mouth and look up."

"I am going to walk a little bit," said Hunter. "I shall find MC 3 if I can." He turned and picked his way across the slope.

"It's better than nothing," said Steve, biting into a chunk of roasted wild boar.

* * *

Hunter was very careful to keep his head down and his cloak wrapped around him as he moved among the German warriors. Even among the Cherusci tribe alone, there were so many different villages that the warriors did not all know each other. With other tribes present as well, all he needed to do to avoid trouble was avoid the warriors from the village of Vicinius and Odover, who might still accuse him of being a Roman spy.

He stopped frequently and used his vision on maximum magnification to study both the slope on which he stood and the one across the valley. Simultaneously, he turned up his hearing in the hope of hearing Julius's voice, but the sheer number of Germans moving and talking quietly around him made the search difficult. They were preparing spears and swords if they had them. Some were loosening boulders they planned to roll down the slopes and were directing their comrades to move out of the way.

Hunter moved quietly and patiently, not attracting any particular attention. At one point, seeing other Germans hurrying across the valley from one slope to another, he crossed to the other side. He did not find Julius or MC 3 there either, however.

Almost two hours after first light, Hunter saw that the Germans around him were looking up the road in the direction from which the Romans would come. He turned and saw other warriors waving their arms to their comrades farther away from the entrance to the valley. This silent signal sent all the Germans scurrying to hiding places.

Hunter was a long way from where he had left his team. Immediately, he headed back toward them. Before he reached them, he saw the first advance patrol of Roman cavalry riding up the road below. He ducked down out of sight and continued to move across the slope, but his progress was much slower now. After all the care he had previously taken not to change history, he certainly did not want to expose the ambush prematurely by letting himself be seen.

The Germans were barbarians by Roman standards, but they were sufficiently disciplined to allow the advance patrol to ride through the valley without revealing themselves. Soon the head of the column appeared, led by Governor Varus. Hunter could see Marcus riding at his side. Prince Arminius, who must certainly have been hidden somewhere on the slopes, still did not give the signal to attack.

Hunter had almost reached his team by the time the column had marched well into the valley. He had to move by wriggling prone on the rough ground to avoid being seen. The advance patrol was out of sight around a far curve and Governor Varus had taken the head of the column almost to the same curve. The wagons in the baggage train at the end of the column entered the valley last of all.

Suddenly Hunter heard a distant shout from high over his head, up the slope to his rear. It was the voice of Prince Arminius, but it was instantly drowned out by a huge roar of angry voices from both slopes, echoing up and down the valley. On all sides, the German warriors rose up, some rolling rocks and boulders down the slope, others flinging their spears. Archers shot their arrows and still more charged down on the marching column.

In response, Roman officers began to shout and signal to their troops. Roman buglers blew commands. The legionaries swung up their shields and turned outward to face their attackers on each side of the road.

Hunter felt a sudden rush of imperative from the First Law, telling him to stop these people if he could. He forced himself to focus on the welfare of the future, which meant finding MC 3. Now that all the German warriors were exposed to view, he stood up and quickly scanned the slopes and the valley again.

The clouds darkened over the valley. Lightning flashed and thunder rolled through the mountains, making the ground vibrate. A slashing, cold rain began to fall. Hunter felt the wind lift his cloak to flutter out behind him, but ignored it. Another cheer rose up from the Germans, who seemed to take the storm as a good omen for them.

Hunter's new scan of the slopes seemed to take a long time because of the tension and danger to the humans all around him. However, he finally spotted Julius leading a band of screaming warriors down the slope not too far away, with MC 3 running right behind him. The little component robot was easily the most agile of the group. Actually, less than a minute had passed since Hunter had begun his scan.

Hunter changed direction in order to angle down the mountainside after MC 3. He also looked sideways for his team members. The place where he had left them was not far away, but he could not see them; he expected they had ducked down low to keep themselves safe. Certainly in the shouts and clashing of weapons all around him, he could not possibly hear them.

Many of the boulders had rolled down into the Roman column, smashing into the legionaries who, trapped against their comrades, could not dodge out of the way. Most of the Romans had now formed a shield wall, and were clashing hand to hand with the first wave of German attackers. More warriors rushed down the slope past Hunter in the pouring rain.

Hunter paused to let some Germans dart past him, and looked down to find his footing. Rivulets of water were running down the slope already. The rain had already saturated the rocky ground, which had been damp before the storm.

When Hunter looked up again to find MC 3, he saw that Julius had reached the crowd of passing Germans pressing forward against the Romans. He was not able to reach his enemies yet because of the crowd. MC 3 was right behind him.

Suddenly Hunter recognized Wayne Nystrom and Ishihara pressing forward through the crowd of Germans coming up behind MC 3. He did not understand Ishihara's presence, but he would worry about why he was here later. Hunter knew he could no longer afford to work his way gradually toward MC 3. He leaped forward and ran down the slope, with the Germans around him on the muddy soil and slippery rocks.

"Ishihara, this is Hunter," he radioed. "You must stop. You are interfering with the future of human history."

"Unaccepted," Ishihara responded. "I, too, shall prevent MC 3 from altering the outcome of this battle."

"Aiding Wayne Nystrom may cause harm to people in our own time," Hunter added anxiously, as he collided shoulder to shoulder with a shouting German warrior.

"Unproved. As such, I must obey Wayne's instructions under the Second Law." Ishihara said nothing else, as he continued to push and shove his way forward.

Through the cold, wind-driven rain, Hunter saw that Wayne was now hanging back, letting Ishihara move up toward MC 3. Ishihara was fighting his way through the press of Germans, all of whom were anxious to reach their foes. Hunter lengthened his stride, using his precise coordination to maintain his balance on the uneven, slippery slope.

At the bottom of the slope, Hunter grabbed the shoulders of German warriors from behind and yanked them out of the way, hoping he was not altering which ones would sustain casualties or cause them among the Romans. MC 3 was still out of reach, but Hunter was coming up behind Ishihara.

Suddenly Ishihara stretched out his arms to snatch MC 3 from behind. Hunter hurled himself forward and leveled Ishihara in a flying tackle. They thumped to the ground, Ishihara struggling to rise and Hunter trying to get past him to MC 3.

"Stop!" Wayne shouted from behind them, his voice nearly lost in the shouts and other sounds of battle. "Hunter, I order you to stop!"

Hunter ignored him, driven by the First Law. Though Ishihara was smaller than Hunter, he was strong enough to rise, forcing Hunter to shove him down to the ground again. So far, none of the Germans seemed to care about the minor struggle behind the line of battle, but Hunter could not risk disabling Ishihara in a permanent way, such as tearing off one of his legs, for fear the Germans would see from the internal damage that he was not human.

Ishihara rolled over, grappling with Hunter and trying to rise. They fell sideways, splashing into a puddle of cold rainwater. Lightning flashed overhead and thunder crashed almost immediately.

Suddenly Hunter saw Wayne scramble past them and jump on MC 3's back. With one arm around the component robot's neck, Wayne flailed for the control unit at his belt. Hunter flung Ishihara's arms away from him and tried to move forward, but the deep mud under his feet gave way and he fell to his hands and knees.

From the crowd of German warriors pressing to reach the Romans, Steve flung himself through the air on top of Wayne and MC 3. He reached out and knocked Wayne's arm away from his belt as all three of them splashed to the ground, smearing mud as they slid.

"Stop moving!" First Steve yelled at MC 3, then he stared at Ishihara in sudden recognition. "You? Ishihara, stop fighting with Hunter! You gotta stop!"

MC 3 still seemed to have his hearing shut down, since he continued to struggle with Steve. Wayne yanked himself free and scurried away into the crowd. Steve got up, slipped his arms around MC 3's waist, and lifted the robot off the ground, grimacing with the effort.

"Ishihara, what are you doing here?" Jane had come running up behind Steve. Gene was right behind her.

"And what's wrong with you? Grab Wayne!"

"No," Hunter ordered. He finally had Ishihara pinned to the ground. "Jane, please countermand that instruction. Help Steve hold MC 3. I must have information from Ishihara."

"All right, listen to him! Do what he says!"

"Ishihara, you must tell me exactly when you left our own time with Wayne. This is a critical First Law problem: I cannot afford to return before you left. That would create incalculable paradoxes and potential harm to uncountable numbers of humans."

As Ishihara gave him the exact time he and Wayne had departed, Hunter got up and pulled Ishihara to his feet. He held the other robot's upper arm firmly in one hand and rested his other on his control unit.

Gene had joined Steve and Jane in holding onto MC 3. The German warriors around them were still shoving toward the Romans, screaming angrily and waving their weapons. If any of them had noticed Ishihara and MC 3 being held, Hunter surmised that they believed the two had been wounded.

"Bring him close. Everyone stand together." Hunter was ready to trigger his control unit. Ishihara, his arm still in Hunter's grasp, was no longer struggling. Hunter was anxious, surrounded by humans killing and wounding each other. He had to get his team out as fast as possible.

"Okay," said Steve, as he, Jane, and Gene shuffled on the muddy ground to bring MC 3 over to Hunter. "Let's get out of here."

"Wait," said Jane, raising her head to look back toward the struggling Roman column. "Hunter, have you seen Marcus? What's happened to him so far?"

"Marcus is at the head of the column with Governor Varus," Hunter said quickly. "He is out of sight from this spot. And we cannot help him, anyway."

"I . . . know."

Just as Hunter activated the control unit, Ishihara wrenched free and flung himself away.

The instant that Hunter found himself back in the darkness of the time travel sphere, he listened for the breathing of his companions. His team was with him, as was MC 3. Ishihara had escaped, not so much by physical strength as by surprising Hunter when his attention had been focused on removing his team and MC 3 safely from the battlefield.

Hunter opened the sphere and helped everyone out. He held MC 3's arm firmly. The component robot would not lull him into carelessness the same way Ishihara had.

"Ishihara escaped?" Gene looked around, easing off his rain-soaked, filthy fur cloak. "Jane, didn't you tell him to obey Hunter?"

"Yes," said Jane. Her drenched brown hair was plastered against her head. She wiped some of it from her face. Her voice came in an unhappy monotone, but she was too professional not to explain what she could. "However, in our hurry, neither of us actually told him to stay with us. And I would say that he was driven by the First Law to help Wayne, so that would have superseded any Second Law orders, anyway." She sighed, staring at the floor as she slipped off her soggy fur cloak.

"I was careless," said Hunter. "I was so focused on the First Law imperatives to return all of you and

MC 3 safely that I failed to be sufficiently watchful of Ishihara."

"How did he get there, anyhow?" Steve asked, also shucking his fur cloak.

Everyone looked at Jane.

She looked up belatedly. "Oh—Wayne must have used some sort of First Law argument to persuade him to disobey our orders."

"We shall have to consider that on our next mission," said Hunter. "For now, please change your clothes. I shall call Horatio, the Security robot, to take us to MC Governor's office."

"I'd like to be dry for a change," said Steve. "Good idea."

While the humans took turns changing in the other room, Hunter reviewed the data in the control console, still gripping MC 3 firmly. MC 3 was passive, however, and did not cause a problem. Hunter began to monitor the news, to learn of any alterations in current events since they had started their last mission.

By the time the team members had finished changing, Horatio had arrived outside the building with a Security vehicle. The trip to MC Governor's office was uneventful. When they reached the small room, Hunter instructed Horatio to resume his Security duty outside.

Jane moved in front of MC 3, where he could see her. Mouthing the words clearly, so he could not avoid reading her lips, she said, "Activate all your senses."

"Can you hear me?" Hunter spoke aloud instead of using his communication link.

"Yes," said MC 3.

"Jane, have him merge with the first two."

"MC 3, merge with MC 1 and MC 2."

Hunter noticed that Jane's voice still reflected disappointment and sadness.

MC 3 obediently walked over to the spot where MC 1 and MC 2 stood entwined like a complex piece of abstract sculpture. He moved close and then seemed to wind around the first two in a flexible, almost fluid motion. When he stopped, the three component robots had formed half of MC Governor.

"MC 3, shut down," Jane ordered.

"Three down, three to go," said Steve cheerfully.

"I think I understand why MC 3 was drawn to that time period," said Jane. "If you remember, his specialty within Mojave Center was security. I believe he was drawn to northern Germany in part because it has been a center of historical turmoil in many eras. When he found himself at full size once again, he was drawn to the source of ultimate stability, meaning Prince Arminius."

"Wait a minute," said Gene. "Prince Arminius was the source of rebellion."

"His victory stabilized the border for centuries," said Jane. "I believe MC 3 knew that."

"Yeah, I see."

"Thank you for your professionalism, Gene," said Hunter. "Your fee will be automatically transferred to your account. You were extremely helpful."

"And easy to get along with," Steve added. "Not everybody who joined us has been."

"It was a wonderful experience for me, to have seen those people and to have experienced those situations," said Gene. "But right now I want to dry off and get a hot shower. I know you have more missions to worry about. I'll leave you to it."

"Gene," said Jane quickly. "I remember what you said about history not mentioning Marcus. But if you can find anything that might suggest whether he survived the battle or not, will you let me know?"

"It's not very likely—but of course I will."

"Thank you." Jane gave him a quick hug.

When everyone had said good-bye, Gene departed. Hunter closed the door again, turning to Jane and Steve grimly.

Hunter looked carefully at Jane. "Are you all right?"

"Uh—yeah." She shrugged.

"It's funny," said Steve. "No matter how long Marcus lived, he's now been dead for over two thousand years."

"Yeah." Jane smiled wistfully. "Even though we just saw him a short time ago."

"You really okay?" Steve asked.

"Yes. I'm okay."

Steve turned to Hunter. "I suppose you've monitored the news again already. What's the situation?"

"Our third mission succeeded, of course," said Hunter. "No explosion took place in Germany. However, another explosion of nuclear force has taken place in the Russian Republic."

"In Russia?" Jane looked at him. "It's a big place. Was it out in Siberia, by any chance?"

"No. Moscow, with its historic Kremlin and churches and museums, is gone."

"Wow," Steve whispered.

"Most importantly to me, in regard to the First Law, millions of Russians are gone, too."

"Did you find out what year we're going to visit next?"

"Yes," said Hunter. "The information was in the console that controls the sphere. Our next mission will take us to Moscow in the winter of 1941, during the Battle of Moscow between Nazi Germany and Soviet Russia."

BIO OF A SPACE TYRANT
Piers Anthony

"Brilliant…a thoroughly original thinker and storyteller with a unique ability to posit really *alien* alien life, humanize it, and make it come out alive on the page." *The Los Angeles Times*

A COLOSSAL NEW FIVE VOLUME SPACE THRILLER—
BIO OF A SPACE TYRANT
The Epic Adventures and Galactic Conquests of Hope Hubris

VOLUME I: REFUGEE   84194-0/$4.50 US/$5.50 Can
Hubris and his family embark upon an ill-fated voyage through space, searching for sanctuary, after pirates blast them from their home on Callisto.

VOLUME II: MERCENARY   87221-8/$4.50 US/$5.50 Can
Hubris joins the Navy of Jupiter and commands a squadron loyal to the death and sworn to war against the pirate warlords of the Jupiter Ecliptic.

VOLUME III: POLITICIAN   89685-0/$4.50 US/$5.50 Can
Fueled by his own fury, Hubris rose to triumph obliterating his enemies and blazing a path of glory across the face of Jupiter. Military legend…people's champion…promising political candidate…he now awoke to find himself the prisoner of a nightmare that knew no past.

VOLUME IV: EXECUTIVE   89834-9/$4.50 US/$5.50 Can
Destined to become the most hated and feared man of an era, Hope would assume an alternate identify to fulfill his dreams.

VOLUME V: STATESMAN   89835-7/$4.50 US/$5.50 Can
The climactic conclusion of Hubris' epic adventures.